Something must...

"Chris, I need you to come home now," Ashleigh said. She sounded upset.

"Why?" Christina asked, suddenly afraid. "What's wrong?"

"Wonder's in labor."

"But she's not due for another three weeks," Christina cried.

"I know," Ashleigh responded urgently. "I wish your dad and Ian were here. Kevin and Melanie went to the movies, so there's no one else around to help."

Christina's father was in Florida with their head trainer, Ian McLean, working the winter racing circuit. Christina pictured her mother all alone with the aging mare, trying to deliver the foal with no help. She knew Ashleigh must be terribly worried.

"I'll be right there."

Collect all the books in the THOROUGHBRED series

THOROUGHBRED Super Editions

ASHLEIGH'S Thoroughbred Collection

* coming soon

THOROUGHBRED

WITHOUT WONDER

CREATED BY
JOANNA CAMPBELL

WRITTEN BY
BROOKE JAMES

HarperEntertainment
A Division of HarperCollinsPublishers

HarperEntertainment
A Division of HarperCollins*Publishers*
10 East 53rd Street, New York, NY 10022-5299

This is a work of fiction. The characters, incidents, and dialogues are
products of the author's imagination and are not to be construed
as real. Any resemblance to actual events or persons, living
or dead, is entirely coincidental.

Produced by 17th Street Productions,
a division of Daniel Weiss Associates, Inc.

HarperCollins books are available at special quantity discounts for bulk
purchases for sales promotions, premiums, or fund-raising.
For information, please call or write:
Special Markets Department, HarperCollins Publishers,
10 East 53rd Street, New York, NY 10022-5299.
Telephone: (212) 207-7528. Fax: (212) 207-7222.

ISBN 0-06-106607-9

HarperCollins®, 🔥®, and HarperEntertainment™
are trademarks of HarperCollins Publishers Inc.

Cover art © 1999 by Daniel Weiss Associates, Inc.

First printing: August 1999

Printed in the United States of America

Visit HarperEntertainment on the World Wide Web at
http://www.harpercollins.com

❖ 10 9 8 7 6 5 4 3 2 1

For Allegra, in loving memory

WITHOUT
WONDER

"READY, GIRL?" CHRISTINA REESE ASKED HER GRAY
Thoroughbred mare, Sterling Dream. She unhooked
Sterling from the crossties and led her down the long
aisle of Whitebrook Farm's broodmare barn. The mares
munched their morning hay, watching quietly as they
passed by.

Outside, Sterling stepped gingerly over the snow-
covered ground, until Christina tugged her to a halt so
that she could tighten the girth and mount up. The
leather saddle felt cold as ice through Christina's thin
dressage breeches. It had been so frigid recently, it was
hard to believe it was February and spring was actually
on its way.

"Whoa," Christina murmured as she gathered up
her reins and adjusted the navy blue wool cooler that
covered Sterling's dappled hindquarters. She pulled the

1

cooler over her legs, tucking it between her knees and the saddle. That way, neither she nor her horse would get a chill on the twenty-minute hack over to Whisperwood, the farm run by Christina's riding instructor, Samantha Nelson, and her husband, Tor.

Despite the wool cooler, Christina shivered with excitement. This weekend Whisperwood was hosting a two-day dressage clinic taught by Lars Stockholm, her three-day eventing idol. She'd been looking forward to the clinic for months and was secretly hoping that Lars would ask her to train with him down in Florida the next winter. Lars Stockholm had started the Young Riders—a special program for young three-day event riders who hoped to compete internationally. Getting onto a Young Riders team and going to the North American championships was a big step toward becoming an Olympic rider—Christina's ultimate aim. The Young Riders had to be at least sixteen, so she had only one more year to go. Actually, Christina had only just turned fourteen on Christmas day, but in the eyes of the United States Combined Training Association—the USCTA—she was considered to be fifteen as of January 1. It was the same way with racehorses. Each Thoroughbred officially turned one year old the January 1 after it was born, no matter what month it had really been born in.

Christina nudged Sterling forward, down the wide tractor road between the two back pastures. The mare responded willingly, her head cocked and her ears pricked toward the big oval training track down the hill to their left. Though it was early morning, everyone at Whitebrook Farm, the Thoroughbred breeding and training farm owned by Christina's parents, Ashleigh Griffen and Mike Reese, was already hard at work. She could just make out the chestnut filly, Missy, jogging around the far turn, with Christina's cousin, Melanie Graham, aboard. Suddenly Missy came to a complete standstill, throwing Melanie up onto her shoulders. Christina chuckled. Missy's full name, Mischief Maker, was entirely appropriate for her, and her cousin had her work cut out for her—the two-year-old was a handful. Christina had broken Missy to a halter and lead line, and she had almost lost her patience more than once. But Melanie seemed to have a knack with problem horses, so when Missy was ready to begin her race training, Ashleigh and Mike had assigned Melanie to exercise-ride her.

"Don't watch, Chris. It might give Sterling ideas."

Christina turned at the sound of her mother's voice. Ashleigh was riding her favorite mare, Ashleigh's Wonder, bareback, just inside the snow-dusted pasture. She looked like a little kid with her blue-jeaned legs dangling around Wonder's bulging sides and her long brown hair tucked into her old jockey's cap. Wonder seemed happy, too, with her head up and her ears pointed eagerly forward. Her blaze and four white stockings were striking against her coppery chestnut coat, which gleamed from over twenty years of special

3

attention and warm Kentucky sunshine. If Christina focused on the mare's finely chiseled head and elegant neck, she could almost see the younger Wonder, the racehorse that stood proudly in the winner's circle with Ashleigh in so many of the framed photographs scattered around their house. But when she looked at the broodmare's back, swayed from years of carrying foals, Christina found it difficult to believe that Wonder had once been the proud winner of the Kentucky Derby.

"She looked so bored in her stall that I decided to take her on a little hack," Ashleigh explained as Christina walked Sterling over to the pasture fence. "I know what it's like to be pregnant—you feel fat and lonely. I don't want her to get depressed."

Christina laughed. "Wonder can't be lonely, Mom. You practically live in her stall."

In fact, Ashleigh had been by Wonder's side ever since the mare was born at Townsend Acres, the huge Thoroughbred farm where Christina's grandparents had once worked. At birth Wonder had been sick and weak. If Ashleigh hadn't looked after her until she was strong, Wonder would have died. Then, when no one thought Wonder would ever even race, let alone win, Ashleigh stood by her, eventually becoming a jockey and riding her to victory herself.

"I don't make very good company, though," Ashleigh said. "Wonder's happiest when she has a foal at her side. I just wish this foal would hurry up and get here."

"Only a few more weeks," Christina said. Wonder

had been bred first, so her foal would be the first of the season.

"I can't wait." Ashleigh smiled and ruffled Wonder's coppery mane fondly. "Have a nice ride!" she added before squeezing her legs gently to urge Wonder on. Christina watched her mother ride away, trailing her fingers along the chestnut's hindquarters in a familiar caress. Obviously Ashleigh had forgotten all about Christina's clinic with Lars Stockholm. But Christina didn't mind—she was used to her mother's absent-mindedness. Ashleigh had been this way ever since she had decided to breed Wonder one last time. Wonder was like a member of the family, so her last foal was bound to be foremost on everyone's minds, especially Ashleigh's. In the last months of Wonder's pregnancy Christina's mother had spent so much time fawning over her favorite mare, she didn't have time for much else.

Christina shrugged as she pushed Sterling into a jog. *It will get better after Wonder's foal is born*, she thought.

"You must talk with the horse using your seat, your legs, and your hands. Your body is the language you must use to communicate what you want."

Christina's eyes followed Lars Stockholm as he lectured from the center of Whisperwood's large indoor ring. Even though his hair was gray and his face was lined and weather-beaten, Lars moved with the grace of

5

a gymnast. Christina could almost see the invisible horse beneath him as he demonstrated what he was trying to explain.

"Dressage has to be a joy for the horse as well as the rider. Only then can it be elevated into art."

Art? Christina had never thought of dressage as being art before, but she understood exactly what he meant: the moment of suspension when a horse trots in place in a piaffe, or the dainty steps of a pirouette. A dressage horse could move as lightly as a ballerina, though the average horse weighed about a thousand pounds more.

"If you use your aids too harshly, if your legs are always nagging and your hands are always taking, it is like you are screaming at your horse. He will be like a teenager. He will tune you out and communication will be broken," Lars continued, his arms pantomiming the pulling apart of a cord. "You must be precise, always asking the same way. Then the horse will look to your aids with eagerness instead of dread."

Christina caught her friend Parker Townsend's glance as he rode by on his bay English Thoroughbred, Foxy.

"Like a teenager, huh?" Parker murmured, his gray eyes sparkling.

Christina smiled, but she was concentrating, striving for the pureness of communication with Sterling that Lars had described. She felt her senses sharpen. Instead of dictating, she was feeling the rhythm, feeling the stretch of Sterling's gaits. She listened, softly encouraging Sterling when the moves became more difficult and the mare grunted with effort. The dust from the arena left her lips chalky and dry, but when Sterling hit her tempi changes—switching her leading leg every other stride at the canter—Christina wouldn't have traded that moment for anything. She had tried tempi changes off and on for the past year with no luck, and now it was as if she had accomplished a year's worth of training in only one lesson. *What would it be like to train with Lars every day?* she wondered.

"Good, good," Lars said. "Now let her rest. Tomorrow we'll do more." Christina brought Sterling back to a walk and loosened her reins. She reached up to pat Sterling's neck. "That mare, you and she make good partners, no?" Lars called.

Christina nodded self-consciously, her muscles still quivering from the adrenaline rush. Sterling brought her muzzle around, her dark eye unblinking as she waited for Christina's next command.

"And how old are you, Christina?" Lars asked. Christina's heart lurched. Was he thinking what she hoped he was thinking?

"Fifteen by USCTA standards," she said, trying to keep her voice from wavering.

"Very good, very good," Lars answered. But he didn't say anything more.

"Come on, girl. Let's cool you off," Christina murmured. She reached down to stroke the mare's shoulder, and Sterling stretched out her neck with a snort.

When the clinic was finished for the day and the last trailer had disappeared down the road, Christina left Sterling happily slurping up a warm bran mash with sliced carrots and apples. She paused at Foxy's stall, where Parker was still settling his mare down for the night.

"You and Foxy looked really great today."

Parker's gray eyes were soft as he patted Foxy's shoulder. "It's almost like she's starting to read my mind."

Christina nodded her head. She felt that way about Sterling, too. "I'm going up to the house to change." Samantha had invited them both to stay for supper. Lars would be there, too, and Christina was eager to listen to anything and everything he had to say.

Parker took a brush out of the grooming box that hung over Foxy's stall door. "I'll be up in a minute—don't you dare start dinner without me!" he warned.

"Don't worry," Christina called with a laugh as she hurried down the aisle. "We will."

"What a feast," Lars Stockholm exclaimed as he reached for a slice of Tor's homemade bread.

"It's not every day that we have an Olympic medalist for dinner." Samantha smiled as she tucked an unruly strand of red hair behind her ear.

Lars waved his fork in the air. "Ah, that's ancient history. The young people I am working with in Florida, they are the future of this sport."

"How many students do you have?" Parker asked, turning his salad white with dressing.

"Eight at the moment. We have to eat in the barn, the house is so crowded," he joked.

"They all live with you?" Tor asked.

"Only in the winter, when we are in Florida. The rest of the time they are at home with their families."

"What do these kids do about school?" Samantha asked.

"They have their lessons with my wife. She home-schools them."

Christina kept quiet, listening intently. Suddenly Lars's light blue eyes focused on her. "You and your mare show great promise. If you would like to come to Florida, I think maybe we could find a corner to squeeze you into."

The telephone rang at that moment, but the sound barely registered on Christina as his words sank in. *Lars Stockholm is inviting me to Florida to be one of his students!*

"Christina, it's for you," Samantha said, holding her hand over the mouthpiece. "It's your mother."

Christina pushed back her chair, wondering if her mother had forgotten she was staying at Whisperwood for dinner. She turned her back to the table as she picked up the phone. "Hello?"

"Chris, I need you to come home now," Ashleigh said. She sounded upset.

"Why?" Christina asked, suddenly afraid. "What's wrong?"

"Wonder's in labor."

"But she's not due for another three weeks," Christina cried.

"I know," Ashleigh responded urgently. "I wish your dad and Ian were here. And Kevin and Melanie went to the movies, so there's no one else around to help."

Christina's father was in Florida with their head trainer, Ian McLean, working the winter racing circuit. Christina pictured her mother all alone with the aging mare, trying to deliver the foal with no help. She knew Ashleigh must be terribly worried.

"I'll be right there."

2

"JUST DROP ME OFF HERE," CHRISTINA SAID ANXIOUSLY AS Parker turned into Whitebrook's driveway.

"I don't mind coming in if you need help." Parker's hand wiggled the gearshift lever as he waited for her reply.

"Don't worry," Christina answered. "I'm sure the vet is on her way."

Parker looked undecided.

"Really, it's okay." Christina said, opening the truck door. "Go back to dinner so you can fill me in on everything Lars says. If Wonder's really in labor, I bet she'll deliver fast. Maybe Mom can even drive me back when it's over."

"Okay," Parker said. "But please call if you need help."

"We will. Thanks again for the ride." Christina

11

closed the door and hurried up the drive to the barn. She'd left Sterling at Whisperwood for the night, since she would be riding in the clinic the following day, too. At least she had one more day to find out if Lars Stockholm was serious about taking her on as his student.

The barn door rolled open in front of her as Parker drove off.

"Christina?" Ashleigh was a black shadow in the lighted doorway.

"Coming," Christina called. When she saw her mother's face, all thoughts of the clinic faded from her mind. "How is she?"

"I don't know," Ashleigh said, striding down the aisle toward Wonder's stall. Christina almost had to jog to keep up. "She's definitely in labor, but nothing is happening yet."

"Who's on duty tonight?"

"Joe was supposed to be, but he had a migraine, so I sent him home after feeding time."

"Did you call Dr. Lanum?"

"She and Dr. Seymour are both out of town, and the vet who's covering for them hasn't returned my call." Ashleigh's voice got soft as she ducked under the webbed stall guard hanging across the door to the big foaling stall. "Hey, Wonder, is that baby ready to come, girl?"

Wonder was standing in the center of the stall with her head hanging down. Even though the air in the barn

12

was cool, Wonder's copper-colored neck and flanks were darkened with sweat. The top half of the mare's tail was wrapped in a white bandage in preparation for the birth. Wonder swished it as though invisible flies were tormenting her.

Ashleigh leaned against Wonder's neck, holding her hand under the mare's jaw to check her pulse. Wonder's normally placid gaze seemed pained, and she jerked her head away from Ashleigh, biting at her side.

"She isn't colicking, is she?" Christina asked. When horses had bad pains from gas or food blockages, they bit at their stomachs the way Wonder was doing.

"Not likely. You can see the labor contractions." Ashleigh rested her hand lightly on Wonder's heaving flanks. "Keep it up, girl. You know what to do."

Most mares got nervous when they were foaling, and usually it was better to leave them alone. But Wonder seemed comforted by Ashleigh's voice. She blinked her dark eyes and sighed. Her sigh turned into a groan, however, as another contraction rippled through her.

Ashleigh turned to Christina. "Fill one of the metal buckets with hot water and disinfectant. And bring the box of latex gloves in case I have to check whether the foal is in the right position."

Christina jogged to the tack room, eager to help. She had witnessed lots of births, but the vet was usually there to assist. Would she and her mother be able to help Wonder if something was really wrong?

"Her water just broke," Ashleigh said when Christina came back. "The foal should be here in the next twenty minutes." Wonder was still standing, her head down, her breath coming in painful rasps. The bedding beneath her was soaking wet.

"Hold on, I'll get a pitchfork," Christina said, and dashed out into the aisle again. She knew the foal could could catch a chill if it was lying in wet bedding. Ashleigh led Wonder forward a few steps while Christina took out the damp straw.

"You're almost finished," Christina heard her mother murmur as she stroked Wonder's blaze.

Wonder tossed her head restlessly and began circling the stall, biting at her flanks. Christina ducked under the stall guard, thinking that maybe if she was out of the way, Wonder would just relax and give birth.

"It's all right, girl. You've done this before," Ashleigh crooned. She caught Christina's worried glance. "I wish she would just lie down before she wears herself out." She was gripping Wonder's leather halter so tightly, her knuckles were white.

"Don't worry. Like you said, Wonder's an experienced mom. She knows what she's doing," Christina answered. "So, who do you think is going to win the bet?" she added, trying to ease the tension. Melanie had come up with the idea of betting on what color the foal would turn out to be. The winner wouldn't have to do dishes for a week. Christina bet the foal would be black like Jazzman, its sire. Melanie hoped for liver chestnut,

14

her favorite color. Her father thought it would be a bay, but Ashleigh was holding out for another coppery chestnut, like Wonder.

Her mother glanced at her. "At this point I don't care who wins. All I want is a healthy foal."

Wonder was pawing the ground now, sniffing the bedding. Christina gasped when the mare dropped onto her knees.

"It's okay," Ashleigh said, cracking a thin smile. "She's lying down to deliver." She sorted through the stuff Christina had brought from the tack room. "Where's the iodine?"

Her mother hadn't asked her to bring any iodine, but Christina didn't say anything. She raced back to the medicine chest and found the brown bottle and a little plastic bowl to pour it into. The foal's broken umbilical cord would be dipped into the bowl of iodine to kill any germs that might cause an infection.

When she got back to the stall, Wonder was standing up again. She was breathing harder than ever, her ears flicking back and forth, her neck mottled with sweat.

"Why did she get up again?" Christina gasped.

Ashleigh shook her head, biting her lip as she checked her watch. "It's been ten minutes. We should be seeing a foot soon."

Christina remembered the diagram in the horse book her mother had given her years before. It showed how a foal comes out: front feet first, nose between its knees, like a diver.

After another ten minutes watching Wonder lie down, get back up, and pace the stall miserably, Christina was going crazy with helplessness. Wasn't there something she could do?

"Do you want me to call the vet again?" she offered.

"Yes. Please," Ashleigh said. "Tell them her water broke twenty minutes ago."

The woman at the vet's answering service kept calling Christina "hon" while she explained that the vet probably wasn't answering his beeper because he was on another call.

"Well, when he phones in, please tell him that there's an emergency at Whitebrook Farm!" Christina told her.

"The answering service says they're trying to get hold of him," Christina reported when she returned to Wonder's stall. The mare was down again, lying on her side with her head up. Her nostrils were flared as though she'd been running hard, and Christina could tell she was getting tired.

Ashleigh stood up from her crouch behind Wonder's shoulder. "We're running out of time. If the foal doesn't show soon, I'm going to have to reach in and check its position."

Christina recognized the note of panic in her mother's voice. "If the foal's trying to come out backward, you can turn it around, can't you?" she asked.

"I can try," Ashleigh said. But she didn't sound very confident.

Wonder groaned as she thrust her front legs out again and thrashed with her back legs. It was a few seconds before she had the strength to jockey herself into a standing position once more.

Ashleigh hurried down the aisle to get scrubbed up and ready. Christina kept her eye on Wonder as the mare paced the stall. Wonder's eyes were tearing, as if she were crying in pain. She lowered her head and sniffed the straw, her knees buckling as she prepared to go down once more. But Ashleigh called out to her, and Wonder's head jerked up again.

"Keep her in the center of the stall," Ashleigh murmured to her daughter. Obediently Christina ducked under the stall guard and grasped Wonder's halter. "Talk to her, and don't make any sudden movements. She might kick me by accident."

Christina couldn't imagine Wonder's kicking anyone, let alone her mother. But she did as she was told, massaging Wonder gently behind the ears as Ashleigh pulled on the latex gloves. Wonder flinched but stood patiently still as Ashleigh began to check the foal's position. The mare's breaths came at such irregular intervals, and it was obvious to Christina that she was in a lot of pain.

It was all Christina could do to remember to breathe herself as she waited for Ashleigh to say something. *Anything.*

"Uh-oh," Ashleigh exclaimed under her breath.

"What?"

"I can only feel one leg. The other one must be caught up somewhere," Ashleigh answered. "Easy, girl. I'm going to try to untangle it. Watch her eyes, Chris."

Christina focused her attention on Wonder's head, knowing that if the mare was going to react, it would show in her eyes first. But Wonder stood steady, her eyes barely flickering as the next contraction rolled through her. Then Wonder's head shot up and her eyes rolled sideways, showing their whites.

"I think I'm getting it—ow!"

"What's wrong?" Christina asked anxiously.

"She stepped on my foot," Ashleigh called back. "It's all right."

"Sorry," Christina said. "Did you get it?"

"I can't tell," Ashleigh answered. She dropped her hands and took a step back. "Let her go now."

As soon as Christina backed up, Wonder dropped forward onto her knees with a groan. Her sides shuddered in another contraction before she collapsed in the straw once more, her legs outstretched and rigid.

Christina looked at her mother with alarm, but Ashleigh was already down on the floor beside Wonder.

"Okay, girl, it's up to you now. Come on," she coaxed.

19

Wonder pressed her head flat against the straw, her eyes squeezed shut with effort. Her nostrils flared with each labored, whistling breath. To Christina, it looked as though she were dying.

"What's she doing?" she cried softly, so as not to frighten the mare—even though Christina was frightened herself.

"I think I can see the hooves," her mother answered quietly. She pushed Wonder's long, silky tail aside, and Christina circled around for a better view. Sure enough, two tiny hooves were sticking out. Christina held her breath and felt her mother clutch her hand as they watched Wonder's body strain, unable to do anything to help.

"Is that its nose?" Christina held her breath as another contraction pushed the foal out even further. "Oh, my gosh—you're doing it! Good girl, Wonder." Her mother squeezed her hand even tighter as they waited.

Wonder gave a final push, and the foal's back legs slid out. Christina stared at the wet bundle crumpled in the shavings. She held her breath, desperately searching for some sign of life, but the foal didn't move.

Wonder brought her nose around and sniffed the still body tiredly.

"It's all right, Wonder," Ashleigh crooned. "You rest now. We'll get him all cleaned up for you." She glanced up at Christina. "Hurry, Chris! Get the towels," she ordered, and Christina scrambled to her feet. "Wonder's too weak to lick him off—we need to get his circulation going." Ashleigh lifted the foal's head and began clearing the mucus away from its nostrils.

When Christina ducked back under the stall guard with a pile of clean towels, Ashleigh snatched one out of her hands. "Okay—we need to rub him all over," she said, briskly massaging the foal's chest with the towel. "It will help him start breathing."

Christina squatted next to the little heap of wet fur and starting rubbing, softly at first, then harder as she followed her mother's lead. The foal was so tiny and delicate, it was hard to believe that one day he would grow up to be a big and powerful racehorse. She jumped when she felt the foal's pulse fluttering beneath her fingers.

"I can feel his heart beating!" she cried.

"And we want to keep it that way," Ashleigh said hastily. "Quick, do his legs, too."

Christina kept rubbing. *Breathe,* she commanded silently. *Breathe!*

She heard her mother swear under her breath. "We're running out of time. I'm going to try mouth-to-nose. You keep working on his body."

Ashleigh rearranged the foal's tiny head so that it was aligned with his neck. Then, using one hand to hold his head and the other hand to cover one nostril, she lowered her mouth until it looked as though she were kissing his little muzzle.

Christina could feel his chest rise slightly beneath her hands as Ashleigh blew air into the foal's nostril. "I

21

think it's working," she reported to her mother.

Ashleigh took a breath and brought her head down again and again, blowing every two seconds. Christina's rubbing took on the same rhythm as she traveled down the foal's little legs, only as large as her arms. When she was halfway down his right hind leg, a movement caught her eye. For a moment she wasn't sure she'd actually seen it, but then it came again.

"His tail twitched," she whispered.

Ashleigh rocked back on her heels and waited. They watched as the foal's downy chest rose once, then twice. And then it began to rise and fall with increasing regularity.

The colt's fuzzy brown eyelashes fluttered. He looked up at Christina with amber-colored eyes and nickered plaintively.

"He's perfect, Mom," Christina whispered, her heart bursting with relief. She glanced at her mother, but Ashleigh was catching her breath, her hands on her knees, her head bent low. She looked exhausted.

Then Wonder nickered, too, throaty and low—her special mother voice. The colt pricked his little ears and flailed his legs in the shavings, desperately struggling to stand up. He stopped a moment to rest, his front legs propped in front of him and his muzzle on one knee. Wonder nickered again, and this time the colt answered, as if to say, *Hold on, I'm coming!*

As Ashleigh moved to Wonder's side the mare lifted her head, softly breathing in the scent of her new foal.

"You've got to get up now, girl," Ashleigh coaxed.

"Your baby needs to nurse." She tugged on Wonder's halter, and the mare thrust her legs out in front of her with a grunt. The little colt twitched with surprise and scrambled awkwardly to his feet just as Wonder heaved herself up. The umbilical cord broke, and Ashleigh rushed to dip it in iodine.

Christina watched the little foal sway back and forth only inches in front of her. He was smaller than most new foals, since he'd come early, but his eyes were bright and curious. Even in this fragile newborn, Christina could see the defined slope of the shoulder and hindquarters that marked a Thoroughbred.

"He's so beautiful," Christina murmured. "Look at his star." The white hair on the foal's forehead looked as though someone had painted a rough heart between his wide-set eyes.

Wonder nudged the foal's shoulder tenderly, and the foal bobbed his head. Then he took a step toward his mother on wobbly legs, stretching out his neck and hunting for her udder.

Christina heard the foal's hungry sucking sounds as he began to nurse. Wonder sighed tiredly, and Ashleigh reached up and put her arms around the mare's muscular neck. She didn't say a word, but tears of relief were streaming down her face.

Christina squeezed her mother's arm and ducked under the stall guard to call her father in Florida. It would also give Ashleigh a chance to get to know Wonder's new baby on her own. He was small and weak, but he was still Wonder's foal, and he would always hold a special place in Ashleigh's heart—that much Christina was sure of.

By the time Christina had finished calling her father and Samantha, the substitute vet had finally arrived. Ashleigh held Wonder, stroking her white blaze, while he examined the foal. Christina stood outside the stall, watching.

"Well, he seems all right for an early foal," the vet said. "I've given him his shots. But I'd keep an eye on him, and the mother, too. The birth's taken a lot out of them both."

Christina glanced at her mother, who was smiling politely at the vet's words.

"We'll do that," she said softly, still stroking Wonder's face. "Thank you."

The vet ducked under the stall guard, and Christina stepped out of his way as he strode to his truck.

Ashleigh came out of the stall and stood side by side with Christina as they watched the mare and foal. It was amazing what a difference an hour could make. When the colt was first born, he'd been all bones and wet fur. Now that he was dry, he looked less like a scarecrow and more like a plush toy with fuzzy soft hair. He reminded Christina of a clown on stilts as he wobbled on legs that were too long for his body. It seemed incredible that he could stand at all, since his still-soft hooves were only as big around as a half-dollar. But he was determined, spreading his legs for balance as he hunted for milk. Whenever he strayed too far, overshooting Wonder's udder and trying to suck on her tail, Wonder would patiently back away, then put her muzzle on the colt's hindquarters to guide him in again.

"How does she know what to do?" Christina marveled.

"Instinct," Ashleigh said. "Wonder was just as good a mother with her first foal as she is with him."

"I'm glad everything turned out okay," Christina said sincerely. "It's a good thing you knew what to do to help her along. I don't think we could have waited for the vet."

"You're probably right," her mother replied. "Besides, that vet was one of those types who seem more comfortable outside the stall than in." Ashleigh rolled her eyes. "I'll be glad when John Seymour is back in the office on Monday."

The colt waggled his tail, nursing eagerly. "I can't believe he's walking around already, and this morning he wasn't even *here*!" Christina exclaimed.

"It doesn't seem so long ago that I was watching Wonder nursing with her mother," Ashleigh said. "I was just a little bit younger than you."

"Have you thought of a name for him yet?" Christina asked.

"No, not yet. It's getting harder and harder to come up with ones that aren't already in the Jockey Club registry."

"It would help if we knew what color he was really going to be," Christina said. Except for the white star, the colt was covered in mousy brown baby fur that would fall out as his real coat grew in.

"Anyone home?"

Christina could hear the outside door roll open and feet running down the aisle. Kevin McLean and Melanie Graham were back from the movies. When Wonder had gone into labor, Ashleigh had arranged for Samantha to pick them up.

"Oh," Melanie exclaimed, sliding to a stop outside the stall. "Look at him!"

Wonder moved so that she was between the foal and the door, protecting him from danger.

"We're not going to hurt your baby," Samantha said, coming up behind Melanie. "We just want to drool over him."

Ashleigh smiled. "Thanks for picking the kids up, Sam."

"Anytime." Samantha ducked down so she could see the colt between Wonder's legs. "Is everything all right?"

Ashleigh sighed. "I think so. I wasn't so sure an hour ago."

"He looks okay, for a little one," Kevin said. He had climbed on the door of the stall next door and was peering through the bars. The expression on his face made him look a lot like his father, Ian.

"Well, if he'd been any bigger, he might not have

come out at all. He had trouble enough as it is." Ashleigh rubbed her forehead and added, "Christina was a huge help."

"Mom had to give him mouth-to-nose—it was pretty awesome," Christina said, glancing at Ashleigh with pride.

"I think it's time for a hot shower and bed," Samantha said, pulling Ashleigh away from the stall. "Do you want me to stay over so I can check on them during the night?"

Ashleigh smiled. "No, thanks. Not when you've got company. I'll be fine now that the kids are home."

"I can do the first shift if you want," Christina offered.

"I don't mind staying," Melanie said.

Ashleigh looked at Wonder standing guard over the colt. The mare held her head low as the foal began to nurse again, her ears limp. Ashleigh had prepared a warm bran mash for her and piled hay in the manger, but Wonder hadn't touched the food. She was tired.

"I think what Wonder needs right now is a little time to be alone with her baby," Ashleigh told the girls. "Let's all go inside and make hot chocolate."

"To celebrate," Christina said, smiling at her mother. Ashleigh put her arm around her daughter's waist and squeezed. "To celebrate," she agreed.

4

ON SUNDAY MORNING CHRISTINA WOKE UP EARLY AND dressed for the second day of the dressage clinic at Whisperwood. A smile crossed her lips when she remembered that the next winter she might be part of Lars Stockholm's Young Riders team in Florida.

"What are you smiling about?" Melanie asked, poking her head into Christina's room. Melanie's blond hair was tousled and her eyes blinked in the light, but she was wearing her riding clothes—ready for another morning of exercising the young racehorses.

"I was just thinking about the clinic," Christina said.

"Is that Swedish guy as great as you thought?"

"He's better. You should have seen the way Sterling looked after he worked with us," Christina said as she tugged a red wool sweater on over her head. "And I didn't get a chance to tell you the best part. I think he wants me to go to Florida to be one of his students!"

"Florida?" Melanie's eyebrows shot up. "Why would you want to go there?"

"Hel-*lo*," Christina said, opening her eyes wide. "Florida is warm. It has green grass right now, and a winter show circuit, and some of the best riders in the East!"

Melanie shook her head. "I think you're crazy to want to leave Whitebrook."

It was the same old argument they always had. Melanie had been raised in New York City and was thrilled to be living on a horse farm in the country. And now that she was exercise-riding, with the hope of becoming a jockey one day, she had really become part of the everyday routine at Whitebrook. Christina, though, had never wanted to race, and even though living on a Kentucky Thoroughbred farm was wonderful, she sometimes felt out of place.

"I didn't say I was *going*," Christina said tentatively. "It was just cool that he asked."

"Then congratulations, I guess," Melanie said, smiling halfheartedly.

"I guess." Christina shrugged. "Anyway, Sam's picking me up in an hour to take me to the clinic. Want to go see Wonder's foal with me after breakfast?"

"Definitely," Melanie answered. "He is *so* cute!"

Christina tossed a hair band to her cousin as they headed down the hall to the stairs. "Here, you might want to try this," she told her with a giggle.

"Hey, I already spent, like, two hours doing my hair and makeup this morning," Melanie joked. Christina laughed and elbowed her cousin out of the way as they raced each other down the stairs.

But when they got there, the kitchen was dark and quiet. Where was Ashleigh? Usually Christina's mother made sure they ate a full breakfast, since both girls worked hard with the horses all day. And Ashleigh always drank coffee in the morning. But the coffeepot hadn't even been turned on.

"Mel," Christina said, glancing worriedly over her shoulder at her cousin, "I'm going out to the barn."

Melanie put back the carton of juice she'd started to take out of the refrigerator. "I'll come with you," she said.

Ashleigh was in Wonder's stall when they arrived. She looked even more exhausted than she had the night before.

"What's wrong, Mom?" Christina asked, resting her hands on the stall guard.

Wonder was standing up, dozing in the corner. Beneath her, the little brown foal lay on his side, legs stretched out in the straw, fast asleep. They looked perfectly peaceful.

"Wonder still hasn't eaten anything, and she's hardly touched her water. Look." Ashleigh reached out and pinched the skin on Wonder's neck. When she let go, the skin seemed to stick in a fold for a few seconds before slowly falling back into place. It was a sure sign of a dehydrated horse. Christina knew that nursing mares needed a lot of water. Usually they went through a few buckets a day. "She just doesn't seem herself," Ashleigh added, shaking her head. Christina could tell from the way her mother's eyebrows drew together that she was worried.

A bucket of steaming bran mash stood at Ashleigh's feet. Christina loved the rich smell of the mash—like fresh bread dough—but Wonder didn't seem at all interested.

"Maybe she's just really tired," Melanie suggested.

"That's what I'm hoping," Ashleigh said, fiddling with the strands of Wonder's long mane. But her anxious expression didn't change.

Naomi Traeger, Whitebrook's apprentice jockey and head exercise rider, stuck her head through the doorway of the broodmare barn. "Are you ready, Mel?" she called down the aisle. "We've got horses to work."

"Coming," Melanie called back. She glanced at Ashleigh. "Sorry. I have to go be tortured by Missy. I hope Wonder feels better, Aunt Ashleigh."

"Thanks, Mel."

Christina watched her cousin jog down the aisle and out the door toward the training barn. When she turned back to Wonder, the little foal's head was up and he was blinking at her, his white star shining in the glare of the barn light.

"I'll be right back," Christina told her mother. Then she hurried to the tack room to call Samantha at

Whisperwood. Christina couldn't go to the clinic now, not when her mother was so worried about Wonder. Lars Stockholm would have to wait for another time.

By Sunday afternoon the little colt was up and scampering around the stall. But Wonder was still resting tiredly, her back leg cocked, watching her baby with a glazed expression. Ashleigh had put electrolytes—essential salts and minerals—in Wonder's water, to replenish some of what the mare's body had lost, but the mare had barely sipped from the bucket, and she hadn't touched her hay at all. Despite his mother's weariness, the foal was looking stronger every hour, though his legs were still unsteady. Christina and Melanie laughed when he hopped over a dusty sunbeam and took a nosedive into the straw instead.

"Slow down, little one," Christina said. "You'll wear yourself out."

"Or wear Wonder out," Melanie said. "She looks so tired."

Christina studied the chestnut mare once more. Were Wonder's eyes a little sunken? Maybe it was just the light, Christina decided. She watched the mare's belly muscles tighten as the colt found her udder and started nursing. She could hear his slurping, sucking sounds all the way across the stall.

"Can you believe he's going to be as big as Wonder someday?" Melanie said.

"Maybe even bigger." As Thoroughbreds went, Wonder wasn't very tall. "Hey, you," Christina said, wiggling her fingers at the foal.

The colt peered under Wonder's stomach and gazed cautiously at them for a few seconds before venturing forward to sniff her hand. Christina loved the way the whiskers around his mouth were all curly.

"Look at his milk mustache," Melanie exclaimed.

"You mean beard," Christina corrected. His chin was covered in white rivulets where the milk had dripped.

Their laughter sent the colt scampering back to his mother. Christina could see his pink tongue curling against Wonder's teat as he started nursing once more.

"How does she look?" Ashleigh called from behind them. "Did she eat any of her hay?"

Christina turned and shook her head. "I don't think so."

Ashleigh pressed her lips together and gazed at Wonder with her arms crossed. Christina knew how frustrated she felt. *If only horses could talk and tell you how they're feeling,* she thought.

"That vet keeps telling me it's normal for a mare not to eat much the day after a foal is born. I *know* that, but Wonder hasn't eaten anything at all. I've left about ten messages for Dr. Seymour—he's going to come first thing tomorrow morning."

Ashleigh ducked under the stall guard and went to Wonder's head. The chestnut mare tossed her head and nickered throatily when she saw Ashleigh.

Behind them, the colt let out a little squeal as he darted around Wonder's legs and wobbled over to Christina. This time he walked right up to the door and held his ground as she reached out to stroke his neck.

"Such a brave boy," Christina crooned. She wanted to hug him tight and tell him that his mother was going to be okay, but she knew that would only scare him away.

Besides, the foal didn't know that his mother wasn't always this quiet and lifeless. For the first three months of his life, Wonder would be her foal's best friend and playmate. Once Wonder was feeling better, Ashleigh would turn them out in the pasture, and Wonder would teach her foal how to roll and play. For the foal's sake, Christina hoped the mare would start feeling better fast.

After a minute the foal turned away from Christina, dropping to his knees before stretching out in the straw for a nap. Seconds later he was fast asleep.

She watched his rib cage moving up and down in a steady rhythm. He looked so peaceful and innocent.

"Pass me that bucket of bran mash, Christina," Ashleigh said worriedly, rubbing Wonder's neck. "Maybe she'll eat some out of my hand."

It was like that for the rest of the day. Christina and Melanie filled in for Ashleigh, doing her chores around the farm, every now and then stopping by Wonder's stall to see if there had been any improvement or if they could help in any way.

When she had a free moment, Christina called her father again to let him know what was going on.

"Giving birth is tiring," Mike said reassuringly. "Once she gets a little grain in her, Wonder will get her strength back."

"But she isn't eating, Dad," Christina insisted.

"I'm more worried about the foal, to tell you the truth," Mike said. "He's early—that puts him at a disadvantage."

"He's doing great, though," Christina said. "He's little, but he's really cute, and he's already playing around the stall."

"Well, that's good to hear."

"When are you coming home, Dad?"

"Tuesday," Mike said. "Listen, Chris, try not to worry, and tell your mom to call me later, okay?"

"All right."

Christina hung up and pulled on her boots once more. Outside the big farmhouse, it was already getting dark. Christina looked at her watch. Five o'clock. She would have been all finished with the clinic by now and would just be putting Sterling away for the night in her stall in the broodmare barn. Instead, Sterling was staying at Whisperwood until Christina had a chance to go get her. Parker had promised to look after her, even offering to trailer her back to Whitebrook the next day if Christina wanted him to. Christina missed Sterling, but she was lucky to have such a good friend to look after her horse.

Christina slipped into her parka and hurried out of the house and down to the broodmare barn. Half the barn lights were already off, but the light over Wonder's stall glowed softly. The little colt was playing peekaboo under Wonder's neck, but Ashleigh didn't seem to notice. She was standing by Wonder's side, her hand on the mare's round barrel, frowning at something in her hand.

"What's the matter?" Christina asked.

Her mother held up a thermometer. "Wonder's running a fever."

"Bad?"

"Well . . . it's not good. I'm going to start her on an antibiotic," Ashleigh answered. "When Dr. Seymour comes in the morning he can give her a thorough going-over."

Christina studied Wonder. Her head was low and her bottom lip was hanging down. Christina could see the pinkish gray color inside. It was almost as if the mare were fading right before her eyes.

"Can I do anything to help?" Christina offered.

"I don't think so," Ashleigh said. "I'll see you up at the house."

But her mother hadn't come back by dinnertime. Christina and Melanie made sandwiches and ate them while doing their homework on the living room floor. And

Ashleigh still hadn't returned to the house by the time Christina was ready for bed. She turned off the light in her room and sat in bed looking out the window at the glow from the barn. She wondered if she should go out and see if her mother needed anything, but she was exhausted from all the extra chores she had done that day, and within minutes she had curled up and fallen fast asleep.

5

IT WAS STILL DARK OUTSIDE WHEN CHRISTINA WOKE UP. THE red numbers on her clock radio said 3:58. She was just turning over, glad to have another hour and a half to sleep, when she heard a truck door closing outside. Christina sat up and looked out the window. Ashleigh was walking with someone toward the barn.

Did Dad come back early? Christina wondered sleepily. The floor was cold under her feet as she stumbled to the bathroom. She kept the light off and peered out the window that looked down on the driveway. Dr. Seymour's big white Land Cruiser was parked under the spotlight in front of the barn that housed the mares and foals.

Alarmed, Christina raced back to her room and yanked her jeans on over her flannel boxers. She went down the stairs two at a time, pausing only for a second to jam her feet into her paddock boots and throw a coat over the T-shirt she always slept in before speeding out the door and over to the barn.

"How is she?" Christina asked, stopping short at the sight of Dr. Seymour examining the mare in the open stall. Wonder's head hung low and she coughed once as the vet slid his stethoscope along her barrel.

Ashleigh nodded silently at Christina before continuing to fill Dr. Seymour in. "Her temperature was over a hundred and three when I called you. I was a little concerned when she didn't seem interested in her grain, but what worries me more is that she's barely touched her water. I dissolved some electrolyte powder into her water, but it's not going to do her any good if she won't drink anything."

The foal scrambled around Wonder's tail when the vet moved to the mare's other side.

"Will you keep him out of the way?" her mother said, glancing at Christina.

Christina nodded, crouching down and stretching her hand out, palm up, toward the little colt. "Hey, you. Remember me?"

The colt raised his head, rocking back against his mother before shooting sideways under her neck. Just as fast, the colt changed direction when he bumped into the vet's legs, practically running into Christina's outstretched arms.

"I got him," she said, one arm under his neck and

the other circling his hindquarters as she restrained him. His heart was beating so fast, she almost let him go. "Easy now. I'm not going to hurt you."

"Just keep him in the corner if you can," Ashleigh said.

"What a pretty boy you are," Christina murmured, her voice and fingers massaging away the colt's fear. "When Wonder feels better, you'll go outside and she'll show you all around your new home." She held the foal against her as Dr. Seymour finished examining Wonder. The foal's little body trembled when Christina cleared her throat once, and he stared up at her, studying her face with such intensity that Christina almost burst out laughing.

The vet took a sample of Wonder's blood and gave her another shot of antibiotics. When he was done, Christina let go of the colt.

"Now you can have your mommy to yourself again," Christina said as the colt scampered away to Wonder's side. She was surprised when Wonder didn't answer her baby's nicker as he nuzzled her, searching for her udder. The only sign the mare gave to show she knew he was there was to lift her back, tightening up her belly as he tugged at her udder and began to nurse.

When Ashleigh came back from seeing Dr. Seymour out, she leaned over the stall door.

"Chris, you should still be asleep. But since you're up, would you mind staying out here for another couple of minutes while I use the bathroom and make myself a cup of coffee?"

Christina hadn't even thought about leaving. "Sure. So what did Dr. Seymour say?" she asked.

"He's not sure what's causing the fever, but he wants to run some tests on her blood." Ashleigh rested her chin on her arms as she stared at Wonder. The corners of her mouth were pulled tight with worry, and the circles under her eyes were dark and deep.

"She'll be okay, won't she?" Christina said.

"I hope so, Chris. I really do," Ashleigh answered softly before turning away.

Ashleigh was still in Wonder's stall when it was time for Christina, Melanie, and Kevin to catch the bus for school.

"Maybe I'd better stay home from school today to help," Christina said as they looked in on Wonder once more. The mare was lying down with her legs tucked under her, her nose resting in the straw. Beside her, the colt was stretched out flat on his side, fast asleep. Ashleigh looked up from the thick veterinary encyclopedia that usually sat on top of the barn's medicine chest.

"No. You go ahead to school. Mondays are quiet days. I'll be fine."

"Are you sure?" Christina asked.

"It wouldn't break my heart to stay at Whitebrook today," Melanie offered. "My English test can always wait."

41

"Nice try," Ashleigh said, "but you need to be in school. Jonnie's here, and Dr. Seymour is going to stop by later, and I can always call Samantha and Tor if I need more help."

"Okay," Christina said. "But I'll come straight home on the bus. It won't be the end of the world if I give Sterling two days off in a row."

"I've got practice after school, but I'll relieve you after dinner," Kevin said. "Chances are Wonder will okay by then, though." Christina appreciated his reassuring tone.

"Thanks," Ashleigh said with a thin smile. Christina wished her mother would get some sleep, but she knew Ashleigh was too worried about Wonder to rest. Her head was bent over the book in her lap again before Christina had taken even a step away.

"Try not to worry, Chris," Melanie said when they'd scrambled up onto the bus and slid into their seats. "It'll be all right."

"I know," Christina muttered, gazing at the barn through the window as the bus pulled away. "But Wonder looked pretty bad, didn't she?"

"Well, she didn't look great, but she's a fighter," Melanie said. "Don't forget that."

That's true, Christina agreed silently. *Wonder's pretty old, though. Is she still strong enough to fight?*

School seemed to stretch on endlessly, and it was all Christina could do to sit through her classes, let alone concentrate. She couldn't stop worrying about Wonder.

At lunchtime she called home to talk to her mother, but no one picked up the phone, and the answering machine clicked on. She would just have to keep her fingers crossed and wait until school let out.

Dr. Seymour's truck was by the barn when the bus dropped her off at the end of the driveway. Melanie had gotten stuck in detention for forgetting her gym clothes, so she was going to take the late bus home.

Christina tossed her backpack outside the tack room door and hurried up the aisle. She could hear Dr. Seymour's gravelly voice.

"I think it's time, Ashleigh."

"Can you give me a few minutes?" Her mother's words sounded thick.

"I'll be outside when you're ready."

He was just leaving the stall when Christina got there. She peered inside, gasping as she took in the heart-wrenching scene. Ashleigh was sitting in the straw with Wonder's head cradled in her lap. The mare's breathing was labored and ragged. Wonder's little foal was standing by his mother's tail, looking as small and bewildered as Christina felt. Her heart went out to him.

"What's going on?" she asked, staring at her mother.

Ashleigh gazed up at her, her face smudged with tears. "Wonder's bleeding internally," she told Christina, her voice unsteady. She bit her lip and turned away. "We have to put her down."

"Put her down? You mean put her to sleep?" An involuntary shudder ran through Christina's body.

Behind her, Dr. Seymour cleared his throat. "She's failing fast. It's best we let her go."

What were they talking about? "Wonder's just worn out from foaling, isn't she?" Christina asked hesitantly. She looked back and forth between her mother and the vet. "All she needs is some time to get her strength back, right?"

Dr. Seymour shook his head. "Her blood is full of toxins, and the damage to her internal organs is too great. The mare's body is shutting down, Christina."

Christina looked searchingly at her mother. "But can't we take her to the clinic?"

Ashleigh stroked Wonder's coppery forelock and shook her head. "It wouldn't be fair to make her suffer any longer."

"But what about her foal?" Christina's voice was too loud, but she didn't care. Her mother flinched, but when she looked up at Christina, her expression was set and her voice was cold. "We'll deal with him later."

Christina felt the blood drain from her face at her mother's tone. She jumped when the vet touched her elbow.

"Come on out with me," Dr. Seymour said gently, and nodded toward his truck. "Ashleigh needs some time to say goodbye."

Christina followed him to the driveway and

watched silently as he rummaged through the stainless-steel drawers.

"I became a veterinarian because I loved animals," he said with his back to her. "Best thing I figured I could do with my life was to treat them when they were sick or hurt." He glanced over his shoulder at her as he added, "It wasn't until I was in vet school that I realized I wasn't seeing the whole picture."

What picture? Christina felt like screaming. *Why are you talking instead of helping Wonder?*

"Sometimes the only way I can help a sick animal is to help it die quickly and painlessly."

Christina looked down when Dr. Seymour put his hand on her arm. His fingers were red and his knuckles were chapped.

"I've known your mother for a long time," he continued. "And I know that this decision wasn't easy for Ashleigh. Don't make it any harder on her than it already is."

A lump formed in Christina's throat as the vet's words sank in. She had been worrying so much about Wonder that she had barely thought about what her mother must be going through. Wonder was Ashleigh's horse, and now she was losing her. If anything ever happened to Sterling, Christina wouldn't know what to do. It was the same for Ashleigh and Wonder, if not more so, since they'd had each other for so many years.

Dr. Seymour's face softened. "Why don't you go up to the house?"

Christina didn't trust her voice, so she just shook her head. Her mother needed her.

Ashleigh was resting her cheek against Wonder's forehead when they got back, her loose dark hair covering her face. When Dr. Seymour cleared his throat, she straightened up, shaking her head when she saw Christina.

"I want to stay," Christina insisted before her mother could try to send her away.

Ashleigh nodded as though she was too tired to argue.

"Do you want to move Wonder outside?" Dr. Seymour's voice trailed off. Christina knew he was thinking about how much more trouble it would be to move her out of the barn after she'd been put down.

"No." Her mother's voice was clear and firm now. "I don't want to make her get up."

The vet looked at Christina. "Why don't you take the foal over there so he'll be out of the way?"

Christina nodded and walked quietly over to the little colt. She put one hand on his trembling shoulder and wrapped her other arm around his hindquarters, guiding him away from his mother. The colt didn't struggle, but his heart was beating nervously and his eyes were wide and frightened. Did he sense what was about to happen? Christina hugged him close, trapping him with her arms.

"Shh. It's all right," she whispered softly as the foal squirmed in her grasp.

Dr. Seymour squatted down by Wonder's shoulder. Christina could hear a tractor running in the distance, and voices from the racing barn, where the evening chores were starting. How could everything else be normal when inside the broodmare barn everything was about to change? Her throat got so tight it was hard to breathe as she watched the vet gently run his hands along Wonder's back. Ashleigh's head was pressed against Wonder's, and the mare's ears flickered as Ashleigh began to cry.

The vet pulled the cap off the syringe, and Christina looked away. She stared down at the strands of straw that clung to the colt's furry back and hugged him more closely. The colt shook his dainty head and nickered softly to his mother. But there was no answer. Ashleigh let out a choking, mournful sob, and Christina looked up. Wonder's body was still. She was gone.

Dr. Seymour put the stethoscope in his ears and listened, his hand on Wonder's flank as if he were reassuring her. Then he straightened, letting the stethoscope hang down as he reached out and patted Ashleigh's hunched shoulder.

Ashleigh didn't respond. Her arms were wrapped tight around Wonder's neck and her body shook with silent sobs.

"Mom?" Christina called, her voice cracking.

Still Ashleigh didn't move.

The foal nickered once more and squirmed in Christina's arms, finally breaking free of her grasp and tottering across the stall. It broke Christina's heart to see him looking for his mother, not knowing she was dead. Christina lunged forward to pull him back, but the vet caught the foal before he reached Wonder's side.

"Easy now," Dr. Seymour said as he scratched the orphaned foal behind the ears. "It's going to be rough on this guy," he told Christina gravely. "Let's get him into another stall and I'll show you how to mix up the Foal-Lac."

6

"IF THIS FOAL IS GOING TO SURVIVE WITHOUT HIS MOTHER, someone's going to have to feed him round the clock," Dr. Seymour explained.

"I can do that," Christina said, watching him closely as he mixed up the foal's formula. The vet raised his eyebrows. "I can get everyone to help," she insisted.

They were in the tack room, going through the box of supplies Dr. Seymour was leaving for the foal. Christina knew that if the colt hadn't gotten the protective antibodies from Wonder's first milk, he would be open to all kinds of infections and would surely die. But the colt had nursed for almost two days—he still had a chance, and Christina was determined to do everything she could to keep him alive.

"Make sure it's mixed well," Dr. Seymour instructed. "But wait for it to cool off before you give it to him.

I'm giving you four extra bottles. Always mix more than you think you're going to need—he will *always* be hungry."

Christina nodded, taking the bottle.

"All right," the vet said resignedly as Christina led the way out of the tack room. "Let's give it a go."

When they arrived at the hastily prepared nursery stall—an empty stall next door to Sterling's—the colt was where Christina and Dr. Seymour had left him, huddled in the corner with his legs tucked under him and his nose resting in the straw. He looked tiny and alone in the big stall.

"Squeeze a little bit onto your hand and let him sniff it," Dr. Seymour advised.

Christina crouched by the small colt. "It's all right," she said softly. His ears were pricked alertly, but he looked so pitiful, it was all she could do to keep from crying. "You poor little boy," she whispered, squeezing the bottle's warm, white liquid onto her palm and holding her hand beneath his delicate muzzle.

The foal sniffed the formula curiously and nuzzled her palm, dousing his curly whiskers in the white liquid. He licked his lips and bobbed his head, as if trying to decide whether or not he liked the taste. But he was hungry, and soon he was nuzzling Christina's hand for more.

"Okay, now let him suck on your finger . . . and then slide the bottle's nipple in his mouth," the vet said. "He'll get the hang of it."

Christina let the foal take her index finger between his gums. She could feel the roof of his mouth as he sucked hard on it, but he butted her palm in frustration when nothing came out. Christina slid the bottle into her hand and removed her finger, replacing it with the rubber nipple. The colt began to suck hungrily, Foal-Lac dripping from the sides of his mouth. He was doing it!

"All right," the vet said when Christina smiled triumphantly. "I'm going to go make some calls for your mother, and then I have other horses to see. Call me if you need me."

"Dr. Seymour?" Christina asked, glancing up at the vet.

"Yes?"

"How long . . . how long before we'll know whether he's going to make it or not?"

The vet put his hands in his pockets and cocked his head, thinking. "A week," he said finally. "If he's eating well and seems to be getting stronger in a week, I'd say he has a pretty good chance."

"Thank you," Christina said, and Dr. Seymour turned to leave. Over and over she traced the outline of the foal's pretty white star as he sucked on the bottle. Already his eyelids were drooping, and soon he stopped sucking and drifted off to sleep. The little bottle was still half full. *One week*, Christina thought miserably. *Will the foal even live that long?*

•••

51

Samantha and Tor came as soon as Dr. Seymour called them.

"Where is she?" Sam asked when Christina came out of the orphaned foal's stall.

"In Wonder's stall," Christina answered, tears welling up in her eyes once more.

Samantha gave her a hug. "Oh, Chris. I know how hard this is."

"How's the foal?" Tor said, peering into the stall.

"Well, I gave him a bottle, but he fell asleep in the middle of it," Christina said helplessly.

Samantha exchanged a sympathetic look with Tor. "It's better if you try not to get too attached to him, Chris."

"Why not?" Christina demanded, searching her instructor's face for some remnant of hope. But Samantha's face was full of pity.

"Orphaned foals are hard to keep going. He might not make it without Wonder," Sam explained.

Christina raised her eyebrows defiantly. She was surprised that Samantha would write the foal off so easily.

"It's not just that," Sam went on, glancing at Tor for help.

Tor shook his head. "Some orphans turn out okay, but a lot of them end up . . . well, *strange*. You can replace Wonder's milk, but it's hard to replace the things she would have taught him."

"But he can go out with the other foals when he's big

enough," Christina said, her voice breaking. *Why do they have to be so negative?*

Tor nodded. "Maybe . . . "

"Come on," Samantha said, tugging Tor's sleeve as she led the way down the aisle. "Ashleigh needs our help."

Ashleigh was still hunched over Wonder, just as Christina had left her. Samantha hurried into the stall and began to help her up. Christina had to turn her head, unable to bear the sight of Wonder's body lying motionless in the straw.

"Let us take care of things," Samantha said, wrapping her arms around her friend as she led Ashleigh out of the stall. "You try to get some sleep. The vet said you've been up since yesterday morning."

Ashleigh tried to shrug Samantha's arm away. "I have to decide where to bury her," she said. Her voice sounded far away and her eyes were vacant.

"Okay," Christina heard Samantha say as they walked slowly down the barn aisle. "Show me where you want her, but then *please* go to bed. You don't need to watch them do that."

Tor followed Ashleigh and Sam out of the barn, and Christina hurried back to the foal's stall. She couldn't imagine the sadness her mother must be feeling over Wonder's death. But there, curled in the straw, was Wonder's last baby. Christina understood that her mother was too sad to think of the little foal now, even though Ashleigh had given him his first breath. And Christina was sad, too, but without her, the foal had no one at all.

He was still asleep, but she sat down in the straw next to him, the bottle in her lap, watching him sleep and praying that he would live. For if he didn't, Wonder would have died for nothing.

After waking the foal once to feed him without much success, Christina finally dozed off herself, stretching out beside the fuzzy brown bundle. Once she stirred to the sound of voices and noises echoing down the aisle—Tor and Jonnie taking Wonder away. But Christina fell back asleep, finally waking to the tickling sensation of whiskers nuzzling her hand. The foal had woken up and was sniffing at the bottle. But when Christina sat up and offered it to him, he refused to drink from it. The colt rose shakily to his feet and began to explore the stall. With trembling steps, he ventured into each corner, finally raising his head and nickering plaintively for his mother.

Christina watched helplessly, choking back her tears. The foal was lonely and miserable—of course he wouldn't eat. There was nothing she could do. He would get weaker and weaker, and then he would die.

"Poor baby," Christina heard Melanie say. She turned and saw her cousin leaning over the stall door.

"He won't eat, Mel," Christina explained.

"Want some help?" Melanie offered, opening the door. She sat down cross-legged next to Christina, and when the colt came over to sniff her outstretched hand, Melanie began stroking his back. The colt's knobby knees buckled beneath him, and he nestled down in the straw in front of the two girls.

"He's getting weaker," Christina whispered, clutching the bottle. "He's got to drink more of this or he'll die, too."

Melanie winced. Christina hadn't left the barn since Wonder died, but she knew Wonder had been taken out to be buried. Melanie had probably seen the grave being dug when her bus pulled in.

Melanie ran her fingers down the side of the colt's muzzle, and he lipped it curiously. "Look, he's trying to suck my hand!" she breathed.

Christina remembered what Dr. Seymour had told her to do when she first introduced the bottle to the colt. She had been so eager to get the colt nursing from the bottle, she had just expected him to take it right away, after that first time. But maybe she needed to be more patient.

Christina squeezed the bottle until her hand was covered in the white liquid and wiggled her index finger into the corner of the foal's mouth. Suddenly he opened his mouth and curled his pink tongue under her fingers, sucking eagerly.

"Quick," she told Melanie. "Squeeze the bottle so it runs down my hand."

It was messy, and more formula got on the floor than into the foal, but it was better than nothing.

When the bottle was empty, the foal licked his lips and nuzzled Christina's arm sleepily.

"Do you think he's still hungry?" Melanie whispered.

But the foal flopped back into the straw, exhausted from the sheer effort of drinking. Christina watched the colt's long eyelashes flutter as he slept. She'd seen many foals that were only a few days old cantering across Whitebrook's green pastures, but this one could barely lift his head to eat.

The vet, and even Sam and Tor, didn't think the little foal would make it. *But I'm going to make sure he does,* Christina thought stubbornly. She just had to keep trying.

After a while, Melanie went back up to the house to see if she could be of some help there. So far the foal had drunk only one of the four bottles the vet had left, and that wasn't nearly enough. Christina couldn't leave him now. She wanted to be there, ready with the bottle, whenever he felt hungry again. *If* he ever felt hungry again. She asked her cousin to bring down a sleeping bag and something to eat—she was going to spend the night in the barn.

When the foal slept, she slept, curled in her sleeping bag, with one of Sterling's blankets thrown over both of them. When the foal stirred, Christina sat up and began the slow, messy process of letting him suck the droplets of formula from her fingers.

Once, in the middle of the night, the foal stopped sucking and rested his chin in Christina's wet palm, gazing up at her with sad, amber-flecked eyes.

"Hello, you," Christina murmured lovingly. The foal blinked, twitching his small brown ears at the sound of her voice.

"You need a name. I can't keep calling you 'you,'" Christina whispered softly. The colt bobbed his head, his white star flashing in the moonlight streaming through the stall window.

Why hadn't she thought of it before? *Star*. *Wonder's Star*. It was perfect.

The foal's head grew heavy once more and Christina lowered it gently onto the blanket, curling her body around him protectively. And soon the steady rise and fall of Star's tiny rib cage had lulled her back to sleep.

"Anybody home?"

At the sound of her father's voice, Christina bolted upright. Startled, the little foal scrambled to his feet. She put a hand out to steady him.

"In here, Dad!" Christina called, extracting herself from her sleeping bag.

"Well, look at you," Mike said, unlatching the stall door and letting himself inside. "Come here, Chris." He opened his arms wide, and Christina threw herself into them. A tumult of emotions rushed through her as her father hugged her close. She was relieved to have him home at Whitebrook, but a lot had changed since he'd left for Florida. From under her father's arm, she could see the colt's inquisitive face, the star standing out boldly on his forehead as he peered up at them.

Christina broke away from her father, swiping at the tears that had fallen before she could stop them. "When did you get back?" she said, sniffling.

"Just now. I left Florida as soon as Sam called, and drove all night," Mike explained. He stroked her hair and pulled a tissue out of his pocket. "So, how's the foal doing?"

"Fine," Christina said, already on the defensive. "I named him Star."

Mike took a step toward the colt and reached out for him, but Star tottered away in fright, pressing himself against Christina's legs. She stroked his neck. "It's okay, he won't hurt you," she murmured. "He's my dad."

"Well, Star knows who his new mom is, I guess," Mike said, raising his eyebrows.

"Who?" Christina stared at her dad, confused.

"You."

"Dad," Christina said, holding back a new onslaught of tears as the foal began to lick her hand hungrily, "I don't want Star to die."

Mike studied the foal, his face hard to read. Was he going to tell Christina that Star's chances were slim, just as everyone else had?

"Well, he's still here now, isn't he?" her father said finally. "You keep it up—he's going to be fine." Christina's heart swelled with relief. "Give him a fresh bottle right now, before he eats your hand. I'm going to go find your mom," Mike added.

Christina pushed the colt gently away and followed her father out of the stall to get another bottle from the tack room. She paused at the tack room door and turned to watch her father's retreating back.

"Dad?" she called down the aisle. Mike turned, waiting. "I know Mom's really sad about Wonder. But will you tell her that Star's going to be okay?" Christina asked anxiously.

"Of course I will," Mike assured her.

When Christina came back to the stall with a new bottle, Star sniffed it eagerly and waited for her to squeeze the formula out onto her hand once more. But he seemed unsatisfied with the meager trickle that dripped off her fingertips. Christina guided his mouth to the red rubber nipple, and finally Star latched on, drinking hungrily until the whole bottle was gone.

"Good boy, Star!" Christina said, throwing her arms around him in a milky hug. Her hands and arms were sticky from the white stuff, and her eyes were gritty from lack of sleep, but she didn't care. The colt held still for a second, then squirmed away from her grasp. He shook himself like a dog, spreading his legs wide to catch himself from toppling over. Star was getting stronger, Christina was sure of it.

Jonnie walked by, pushing a wheelbarrow. He dropped the handles and leaned into the stall.

"You can't stay in here all day, Christina," he said, shaking his gray head. "You have school."

"But I have to look after Star," Christina insisted.

"Star?" the stable hand said, smiling. "That's a pretty name."

"Wonder's Star," Christina clarified, and Jonnie frowned, his eyes sad.

"I told your dad I'd feed him while you're at school," Jonnie offered. "But with Ian away and the other mares getting ready to foal soon, we're all going to be extra busy. We're going to have to rely on you and your friends to take care of him the rest of the time."

"We will," Christina promised. "What time is it, anyway?" She felt as though she'd been in the barn for weeks.

"Time to get in the house and get ready for school," Jonnie said. "Go on. I'll feed your little Star."

Christina bundled up her sleeping bag and let herself out of the stall. Star tried to follow her, but Jonnie barred his way, another bottle in his hand. As she hurried out of the barn, Christina tried to block out Star's cries. They sounded just like his plaintive nickers for Wonder the night before—only this time they were for her.

The first week of Star's life was exhausting. Christina stayed with him whenever she could, and she, Melanie, and Kevin took turns getting up every two hours to feed him through the night. Parker finally trailered Sterling back to Whitebrook, and the mare was back in her old stall, but Star's round-the-clock schedule gave Christina hardly any time to ride. Some days she could squeeze in a quick hack, trotting Sterling across the muddy fields surrounding Whitebrook. But more often than not, she had just enough time to groom Sterling before it was time to feed Star once more. At the end of each day Christina was so tired, she fell asleep doing her homework. But each morning when she saw Star standing strong and alert, nickering as she approached his stall, Christina knew her hard work had all been worth it.

On Sunday Dr. Seymour returned to check on Star. Christina held the colt still, waiting anxiously while the vet examined him. First he felt Star's pulse, frowning at his watch. Then he listened to the colt's heart with the stethoscope and peered at his eyes and ears with a miniature flashlight. He took Star's temperature, and finished the examination by drawing blood. Star flinched when the needle went in.

"It's all right, boy," Christina soothed. "I've got you." Star's ears flicked back and forth at the sound of her voice, and the colt let Christina hold him until the vet was done.

"It's remarkable," Dr. Seymour said from where he was crouched by Star's shoulder. He stood up. "I'll run some tests on his blood, but I can almost guarantee it's going to check out fine. He's as healthy as any colt that's been through half of what he has."

Christina could hardly believe her ears. "You mean he's going to be all right?" she asked. She let Star go, and the colt shook himself, stirring up dust in the sunny stall.

"Well, he'll live," the vet said, beaming. "Thanks to you. But the hard part is yet to come. He's an orphan, Christina—they're a lot of work."

"We can do it! Can't we, Star?" Christina cried, rubbing the colt's ears. Star bobbed his head in response and then tottered off to the other side of the stall.

"I'll call with his blood test results," Dr. Seymour promised, opening the stall door. "And I'll be available anytime you need me."

"Thank you," Christina said gratefully. She followed the vet out to his truck and hurried up to the house. She couldn't wait to tell her parents—Star was going to be all right after all!

Christina burst into the kitchen. Her father was standing at the sink, scrubbing potatoes, while her mother grated cheese into a bowl at the kitchen table.

"Guess what?" Christina said breathlessly.

"What?" Ashleigh asked, looking up.

"Dr. Seymour said Star is fine. I still have to bottle-feed him and watch him, but he's going to be all right!"

Ashleigh put the cheese grater down and stared into the bowl on the table. Mike glanced at her and then turned to face Christina. "That's wonderful news, Chris, it really is." He looked briefly at Ashleigh once more. Ashleigh's eyes hadn't moved; she was still staring into the bowl of cheese. Christina had never seen her mother look so distant. *What's the matter?* she wondered silently.

Christina looked from her mother to her father, waiting for one of them to say something.

Mike cleared his throat and dried his hands on a dish towel. "You might want to try taking him outside soon, Chris," he suggested. "I'll give you a hand when you're ready."

"Thanks, Dad!" Christina smiled, relieved that her father was offering to help. Star was going to love being out in the fresh air. "And when the other mares have had their foals, he can go out and play with them," she said excitedly.

Ashleigh stood up quickly and carried the bowl of cheese to the counter. With her head bowed, she brushed past Christina and headed out the kitchen door.

"We can punch holes in one of the weanling halters for him," Mike continued.

But Christina was staring after her mother.

Ashleigh was acting so strange—she'd hardly said a word.

Maybe she just needs time to get over Wonder's death, Christina thought doubtfully. But Star was Wonder's baby. Didn't her mother want to help him?

7

AS SOON AS HER SCHOOL BUS PULLED UP IN FRONT OF Whitebrook the next afternoon, Christina jumped up from her seat, leaped from the bus, and ran to the barn. She dropped her book bag in the corner of the aisle, collecting her long red-brown hair into a ponytail as she hurried into the tack room. Parker was meeting her in half an hour for a trail ride. She had to feed Star, clean out his stall, groom Sterling . . . *I'd better get a move on,* she told herself.

When she arrived at Star's stall, the colt was hunkered in his usual place in the corner, where he lay whenever he was alone. He nickered softly when he saw Christina and scrambled to his feet. Christina unlatched the stall door and rushed to his side. She hated to think that he'd been alone all day, except when Jonnie came to feed him.

Christina had thought of putting Sterling and Star together in one of the large foaling stalls, but she knew it was too risky to try. They were already neighbors, and whenever the colt stretched his head up to sniff Sterling's nose through the bars dividing the top half of the two stalls, Sterling would gnash her teeth and kick out at the wall in warning. One well-aimed kick from Sterling could cripple or even kill the colt. Older horses just couldn't be trusted around foals. Even the broodmares, who would soon be having their own foals, would see Star as a threat to their newborns and turn on him.

When the other foals were older, Christina would try turning him out with them. But for now, Star would have to get used to being alone.

The colt sucked on the bottle, his eyes closed in concentration and pleasure, while Christina went over his furry body with a soft brush. Star was still very small and delicate, and covered in mousy brown fuzz, but beneath the baby fur some bright coppery hairs were beginning to show through. Star was going to be a chestnut, just like Wonder—Christina was sure of it.

When the bottle was empty, Christina kissed the colt in the middle of his heart-shaped star. "Be good," she said. "I'm going riding."

Christina groomed and tacked up Sterling hurriedly, leading her out of the barn and into the late-afternoon sunshine. Just then Parker jogged down the path between the back pastures on Foxy.

"Ready for our trail ride?" he called.

Christina handed him Sterling's reins. "Can you hold her for a second, Parker?" she asked. "I just want to run in and check on Star before we go."

"No problem."

Christina ran back to the tack room, where Melanie and Kevin were sitting on a trunk, cleaning bits.

"Do you guys want to come with us?" Christina asked them, knowing full well what the answer would be. They had both been getting up at five every morning to exercise-ride, and even though they loved it, by the time the afternoon rolled around, riding was the last thing they wanted to do.

"No way," Melanie said. "I sat in enough saddles this morning, thank you very much."

"Me too," Kevin added.

"Well, could you keep an eye on Star while I'm gone?" Christina asked.

"Yes, Mom," Melanie answered with a laugh.

"Don't worry, Chris," Kevin assured her. "Star'll be fine."

"Thanks," Christina said, and hurried back outside.

"What a mother hen you're turning out to be," Parker teased as he waited for her to mount up.

Christina swung onto Sterling's back, stroking the mare's neck to praise her for standing still. "Well, what would you do if he were your colt?" she said, picking up her reins and stirrups.

"I don't know. Keep him in the house, I guess," Parker joked. "My mother would love that!"

Christina laughed at the thought of a colt living inside the spotless house at Townsend Acres. Brad and Lavinia Townsend weren't exactly the most understanding parents around, especially when it came to horses. To them, raising and training racehorses was a lucrative business. Horses were meant to race and win, not to be coddled and fussed over. Luckily Parker's grandfather, Clay Townsend, had a soft spot for horses, too, and he took his grandson's side whenever Parker needed him to. It was Clay who had bought Foxy for Parker, and for Parker's sixteenth birthday Clay had given him his own truck and horse trailer, so he could trailer Foxy to events. If it had been up to Brad and Lavinia, Parker would have been at boarding school, far away from home and without a horse to ride.

They headed out, hacking across the damp green pastures to a sheep farm on the far side of Whisperwood. Sterling snorted at the herds of white sheep grazing in the fields on either side of them.

"Don't be silly, girl," Christina said, letting her heels sink in the stirrup irons as she sat deeper in the saddle. "They're the ones who should be scared—you're bigger."

But it was a toss-up who was most afraid. As soon as the sheep started to trot as a group, away from the horses, Sterling began to canter sideways, her hindquarters shifting from side to side as she tried to keep both flocks in sight.

"Too much angle," Parker said, laughing. "The dressage manual says no more than forty-five degrees for shoulder in."

"Thanks for the tip," Christina said, sitting back in the saddle and easing Sterling down to a walk again. The mare's neck had darkened from silver to pewter from sweat. "I think she needs to get out more," Christina added, patting the mare to calm her down. Because of Star, she hadn't been able to ride Sterling as much, and now she was paying the price.

"You've got to give her more to think about," Parker agreed. "When's your first event?"

"I haven't signed up for any yet," Christina admitted.

Parker looked surprised. "Not even Stony Ridge next month? I thought you were coming with me."

"I was," Christina said. "But I got so busy with Star that I forgot to mail my entry."

"I guess if Foxy and I want company at Stony Ridge, I'll have to bring an entry form to school on Monday so you can fill it out," Parker teased, shaking his head.

"Would you?" Christina said, smiling at him. "That would be great."

When they got to the farm's driveway, they turned around to head for home. Beside the farmhouse, a huge dog was standing on its hind legs, biting at a torn screen in one of the first-floor widows. Christina squinted, trying to figure out what kind of dog it was. The dog came down on all fours and trotted up the driveway to greet them.

"*Maaa.*"

It isn't a dog at all—it's a goat! Christina realized.

68

Foxy and Sterling stopped in their tracks, reaching out their noses to sniff the goat's scent. Sterling's ears were pricked, and she was unafraid.

"I think Sterling likes goats." Parker let out a laugh. "You know, my riding instructor in England had a goat to keep his blind hunter company. They're real trouble-makers, but some horses love them."

"Sterling's enough of a troublemaker on her own," Christina told him. "Come on—I need to get back to Star."

After a few minutes Parker turned Foxy down the path to Whisperwood, where he boarded Foxy full time, while Christina trotted Sterling back home to Whitebrook. As they crossed the farthest field behind the big pasture where the mares were turned out with their foals in summer, Christina caught sight of her mother's red jacket. Ashleigh was kneeling on the patch of freshly turned earth that was Wonder's grave, just staring at the dirt. Christina turned away. *How long is she going to be like this?* she thought sadly as she rode toward the barn.

She leaned forward to hug Sterling around the neck and then dismounted, running her stirrups up before leading the mare into the barn. Down the aisle, a small group was gathered around Star's stall. Christina quickened her pace, a lump forming in her throat when she recognized Parker's father, Brad Townsend, standing with Mike and Melanie.

"It's really too bad about the mare," Brad was saying to Mike. "She was irreplaceable."

Christina nodded solemnly at her father and led Sterling into her stall, untacking her with trembling hands. There could be only one reason Brad Townsend was looking at Star.

Christina had almost forgotten about her mother's old deal with the Townsends; in fact, she'd never thought much about it. Now it was coming back to haunt her. In a contract drawn up when Wonder was only a filly, Clay Townsend had given Ashleigh half ownership of Wonder and all her offspring. The other half belonged to the Townsends. Would Brad Townsend want to take Star away?

Melanie slipped past Sterling's stall, mouthing, "I have to go." She rolled her eyes and jerked her thumb at the back of Brad Townsend's head as if to say, *What a jerk!* Then she walked away down the aisle.

Normally Christina would have had to stifle a laugh, but she was too worried about Star even to crack a smile.

"What a shame," Brad went on. "I've never seen a Thoroughbred so small and shy. He's got *dud* written all over him."

Christina unclipped Sterling's halter and tossed her brushes into the box outside the stall, her blood boiling. She latched the stall door and strode over to where her father and Brad Townsend were standing.

"Star is *not* a dud," she said, glaring up at Brad Townsend.

"Chris," her father warned sharply. Christina's family owed a lot to the Townsends, and she knew it wasn't right to be rude to them. But she couldn't help herself. Someone had to defend Star.

"It's all right, Mike," Brad said, shrugging. "I'm glad she's looking out for the little guy. He'll need it. Who knows—maybe he'll make a nice pet." He thrust out his arm and shook Mike's hand. "Thanks for letting me know about Wonder. My father's still in England, but I'll give him the news as soon as I can. Give Ashleigh my regards."

"I will," Mike said. "Thanks, Brad."

When Brad had left, Christina looked in over the stall door.

"Hi, Star," she called, and opened the door. Star nickered as usual, shuffling out of the corner to greet her. Christina's smile turned to a frown. Though she hated to admit it, Brad was partly right—Star was a little shy. But he was only nine days old. With time, Christina was going to do everything in her power to prove Brad wrong.

"Dad?" she said, turning back to Mike. "Will you help me take him outside?"

"Sure," Mike agreed. "I'll go get a halter."

Christina let the colt sniff the worn old weanling halter until he was sure it wasn't going to hurt him. Then she rubbed it against his face and neck, talking to him all the while.

"See, it's just a silly halter," she said in a singsong voice. "No big deal."

Finally Christina slipped the noseband over Star's

muzzle and quickly drew the halter up over his ears. Star raised his head in alarm, but the halter was on, and there was nothing he could do. The colt shook his head, getting used to the feel of leather against his skin.

"There. It's not so bad, is it?" Christina asked. She clipped a lead line onto the halter, and Mike opened the stall door.

Star peered through the open doorway hesitantly. Christina tugged gently on the lead line, while Mike went into the stall and wrapped his arm around the colt's hindquarters to keep him from going backward.

"It's all right, boy. Don't you want to know what's out there?" Christina asked.

But Star looked frightened.

"Come on," Mike coaxed, pushing from behind. "Let's go."

Step by step they inched down the row of stalls, the broodmares tossing their heads and watching with interest as they passed by.

When they reached the wide opening to the outdoors, Star planted his tiny front hooves and stopped abruptly. His ears were rigid, listening for danger, and his delicate nostrils were flared, taking in all the new smells. The colt rolled his eyes, raised his head, and snorted sharply in alarm.

"Shh, baby. You're fine," Christina soothed. "I'm right here."

"Let him think about it before we go anywhere," Mike advised, relaxing his hold around Star's hindquarters.

Christina stroked the colt's tense neck. She could feel his heart thundering in his chest. "You're fine," she repeated.

To the left, the clatter of hoofbeats rang through the air as Jonnie led one of the racehorses in training down the pebbly path from the paddocks. Star flinched and began to tremble, shaking visibly, as they approached.

"Look who's here," Jonnie called merrily, leading the horse toward them. "Hey, think Missy could use a bath?" he added, chuckling at his own understatement. The chestnut filly had rolled and was covered with dried mud from mane to tail. She was a mess, but she was in high spirits, and when the filly she saw Star, she whinnied gleefully.

"Hold up, Jonnie," Mike called out. But it was too late. Star had had enough. He backed up, skittering sideways in the aisle, and then whirled around, nearly ripping Christina's arm out of its socket. She stumbled after him, frightening the poor colt even more, and he shied away, bumping into a broom that was leaning against the wall and sending it crashing to the cement floor with a loud noise. Star bolted out of the broom's way, nearly landing on top of Christina, and ducked his head under her armpit as if to hide from the world.

She wrapped her arms around his neck. "It's all right, Star. It's all right," she said, though Christina didn't feel as though *anything* was all right.

"Let's get him back into his stall," Mike said. "I think he's had enough for one day."

Together they led the colt back down the aisle. It was easier this time—Star couldn't wait to be back in the familiar shelter of his stall.

Christina unbuckled the halter and rubbed the spot on the colt's nose where the noseband had pressed the hair flat. Star huddled against her and sighed, as if he was relieved to be back in a safe place.

Oh, Star. What are we going to do with you? Christina thought in despair. What good was a horse that was afraid of other horses?

"What that colt needs is a friend," Mike mused, watching them.

"But *I'm* his friend," Christina protested. She was getting tired of hearing people talk about Star as though he had too many problems that were too hard to fix.

"I mean an animal friend—to bring him out of his shell."

Christina stroked the colt's soft nose, waiting for her father to suggest some brilliant solution to all of Star's problems. She was too tired to think of anything. But then an idea hit her, and she turned back to her father.

"What about a goat?" she demanded.

Mike shrugged. "I suppose it's worth a try."

8

FRIDAY AFTER SCHOOL, PARKER PICKED CHRISTINA UP IN HIS truck to drive her out to the sheep farm.

Mrs. Devon, the owner of the farm, was quick to sympathize with Star's plight. "I suppose I could lend you Nana for the summer if you think it would help."

Parker and Christina looked at each other.

"Nana?" Christina said.

Mrs. Devon's doughy face broke into a smile. "There she is now."

The large black-and-white goat came trotting around the corner with a dog dish in her mouth, her long ears flopping. A Jack Russell terrier was close behind her, barking.

"Nana's such a tease," Mrs. Devon said after she'd wrestled the plastic dish out of the goat's mouth. "Fact is, I think she's been bored since my husband died and the grandchildren took the horses. The way she's been tormenting the dog lately, I think she could use a little vacation."

"So she's been around horses?" Christina asked.

"My, yes. She ran the herd all right. Even decided which horse should be allowed to go through the gate first at feeding time. Made sure the old pony got a fair share of the hay in the field, too. She's got a mind of her own."

Christina smiled as she watched Nana untie the woman's shoelace. Maybe the goat would be able to teach Star how to play and have fun, too.

"Go away, you pest. Shoo!" Mrs. Devon hissed, but she was smiling.

"Can we bring her home now?" Christina ventured.

"The sooner, the better," Mrs. Devon called over her shoulder as she ran to rescue the towel Nana snatched from the clothesline.

Parker raised his eyebrows. "Do you think your mom will mind?"

Christina thought of her mother, who had been so quiet and distant lately. Christina had been spending all her spare time with Star, and Ashleigh had hardly even looked at the colt. Then Christina thought of Star, huddled alone in the big stall.

"She doesn't have any choice," she answered. "Besides, it was Dad's idea. Sort of."

Parker pulled on the goat's lead rope while Christina stood in the bed of the truck, waving a carrot. After a moment Nana jumped up to eat the carrot.

"Goats like to be up in the air looking down on things," Mrs. Devon explained. "I think it has something to do with their instincts. You know how wild goats climb rocks so they can see their predators?"

Christina's knowledge of goats was limited to what she remembered from reading *Heidi*. "She won't jump out while we're driving, will she?"

Mrs. Devon was unconcerned. "Good heavens, no. She has more sense than that. Old Nana here used to ride in the back of the truck whenever my husband drove to the post office. The postmistress always had a carrot for her, bless her soul. Just don't drive too fast and she'll be fine."

Even so, Christina rode all the way to Whitebrook facing backward and holding on to Nana's lead line through the truck's sliding rear window. First Nana poked her head through the opening and gazed adoringly at Christina until she had conned the last carrot out of her. Then she dropped to her knees before settling down to watch the passing farms as though she were a tourist on a bus. When they got to Whitebrook, Christina's stomach hurt, she had laughed so much. Something told her it was going to be interesting having Nana around.

"You didn't," Kevin said when Parker stopped the truck outside the mare and foal barn. "Do Ashleigh and Mike know about this?"

"Dad does," Christina said, sliding out of the truck. Melanie came out of the barn. "You got a llama?"

"It's a goat, city girl," Christina teased.

"I thought goats had horns," Melanie explained over their laughter. She stretched up to scratch behind Nana's ears. "She's cute."

"Cute? She's a tank," Kevin said. When he reached up to pat her, Nana butted his arm away. "Whoa," he said, jumping back. "Good thing she *doesn't* have horns."

Parker made a face when he looked at the pile of goat manure in the bed of his truck. "Let's get her out of here before she does any more damage."

But Nana didn't want to get down from the truck. She ignored Christina's tugs on the rope, and lowered her head in warning when Kevin and Parker hopped up to try to push her out.

Christina was beginning to wonder if the goat was going to be more trouble than she was worth when Nana suddenly twitched her tail and leaped nimbly off the tailgate. She trotted over to Melanie with a little bleat.

"I may be a city girl," Melanie said as she held the bucket of grain that Nana had eagerly dived into head-first, "but I'm no dummy."

Melanie used the grain to coax Nana into the barn while Christina ran ahead to Star's stall. The colt was dozing in the corner, but he got to his feet, shaking himself when he saw her.

"Hey, Star. I brought someone for you," Christina told him.

She knelt down, positioning herself beside him with one arm around his hindquarters and the other cradling his chest, to keep him from bolting when he met the goat. "Okay. Bring her in," she called to her friends.

Star's head popped up when Kevin opened the door and Parker and Melanie shooed Nana through it. Christina could feel the little colt's heart pounding in his chest as he grunted and squirmed to get away.

"*Maaa*," Nana called, ignoring Star and trotting to his water bucket. She stuck her nose inside, pulling it out and flapping her lips comically. "*Maaa*." She put her front feet up on the frame of the hay manger that sat like a large trough in the corner. Then she jumped all the way up and lay down in the manger. Christina laughed as the goat surveyed them from her perch.

"Star, this is Nana. Nana, this is Star," Melanie said, giggling.

Star didn't seem amused.

"Let him go and see what he does," Kevin suggested.

Christina rubbed Star's neck before she dropped her arms and backed away. The colt's eyes widened, and he followed, pressing against her legs.

"He won't leave me," Christina said, a little flattered by the colt's attention.

"Then come out here," Parker said. "Give them some space so they can get to know each other."

Star followed her to the door, walking sideways so he could keep an eye on Nana, who was still lying on top of the manger.

"*Maaa*." The two pouches that hung like miniature

rabbit's feet under Nana's chin wobbled when she shook her head. She looked down on Christina and Star imperiously, like a queen from her throne.

"You'll be okay, boy," Christina said, dropping a kiss on Star's velvety nose before backing through the door. She bumped right into her father.

"So you've actually done it," Mike said incredulously. He gazed down at Star, who was pressed up against the door, trembling. "He doesn't look too happy about it."

"They'll make friends with each other," Christina said confidently. "Her owner said Nana loves horses."

Mike shook his head, smiling as if he couldn't quite believe his eyes. "Well, I've got to give you credit for trying. But now you've got another mouth to feed—"

"Don't worry," Christina interrupted. "We can take care of her. Right?" she added, looking anxiously at her friends.

Melanie, Kevin, and Parker all nodded in agreement.

"All right." Mike sighed. "But I haven't warned your mother about this. We don't even have dogs—I'm not sure how she's going to feel about a goat."

"Don't worry, Dad. I'll tell her."

Christina was glad Nana waited until her father left before poking her nose through the bars and chewing on a lead line.

"Look at Star," Melanie said. "He thinks Nana has found something yummy."

Sure enough, the colt had ventured closer to the goat, his nose quivering as he sniffed the air.

Christina grinned. She was betting they'd be buddies in no time. She left Star and Nana with her friends while she went to find her mother.

Ashleigh was watching Naomi and Melanie wrestle with Gomer, an awkward two-year-old colt who had a mind of his own. Gomer could be sweet and docile one moment and standing straight up on his hind legs the next. Naomi had been almost ready to give up on the moody two-year-old, saying he was just too unreliable. In fact, she'd wanted to send him to auction. But Melanie was convinced that Gomer had it in him to be a great racehorse, so she had talked Ashleigh and Mike into trying Gomer in a few maiden races before they made up their minds. Christina didn't know if she'd be as sympathetic toward the colt if he had dumped her as many times as he'd dumped Melanie, but she had to hand it to her cousin for not giving up.

Ashleigh had one foot propped up on the board fence while she watched.

"Better longe him first," she called to Naomi. "Give him a chance to get the bucks out of his system before Melanie gets on." Every young horse at Whitebrook was trained to longe—walking, trotting, and cantering in a circle while attached to a long lead line.

"Mom?" Christina called. "Parker and I brought a goat home. To keep Star company. He was scared at first, but I think he's going to like her—"

"Good," Ashleigh said, cutting Christina off. Her mother looked away, but not before Christina saw her jaw tightening. "I'll get the longe line," Ashleigh called to Melanie.

"Good"? That's it? Christina thought as Ashleigh strode away toward the barn. *Oh, well. At least she didn't object to Nana's coming to Whitebrook.*

By the time Christina had finished up in the barn that night, Star and Nana were eating hay side by side. Star didn't have enough teeth yet to do more than scatter the hay around the stall, but he looked relaxed and content.

When Christina went in to fill up their water bucket, Nana butted her leg playfully and let out a throaty bleat.

Star looked up, his ears pricked. He no longer seemed afraid of Nana, but he was more interested in watching the goat than playing with her. Christina hoped that some of Nana's frisky personality would start to rub off on the colt soon.

Footsteps stopped outside the stall. When Christina looked up, her mother was standing at the door. It was the first time Christina had seen Ashleigh near Star's stall.

"Star really likes her, Mom," Christina said enthusiastically. "Like I was telling you, he was a little scared at first, but I think it's going to work out great."

Ashleigh's eyes flickered quickly over Star before settling on Nana.

"Be sure you keep the bedding picked out. I don't want the barn to start smelling like livestock," she said.

Before Christina could even answer, Ashleigh ducked into the feed room and began to discuss the broodmares with Jonnie. Four of the mares were due to foal that week, so Christina could see why her mother seemed tense and worried, especially after the ordeal with Wonder. Still, Christina wondered why she never seemed to have any time to talk about Star.

By the end of the week Nana had made friends with everyone at Whitebrook. Even George Ballard, the gruff stallion manager who barked at anyone who didn't follow his rules to the letter in the stallion barn, came over to see what all the fuss was about.

"I had a goat once," he admitted, cracking a rare smile as he scratched Nana's neck. The goat was standing with her front hooves braced on the stall door so she could see into the aisle. "Used to hitch her to a little cart." George looked at Star, who was hanging back. "Nice-looking colt. Too bad he's an orphan."

Christina bristled. "Star is going to be just as great as Wonder someday," she said defiantly.

The stallion manager raised his eyebrows, but he didn't say anything else.

WHEN CHRISTINA AND MELANIE CAME HOME FROM SCHOOL the following Monday, Whitebrook's staff were a little less pleased with Nana.

"Can't you do something with that darn goat? Her bleating is driving us crazy," Jonnie said.

Melanie looked at Christina, and it was all they could do to keep from bursting out laughing. Those were the strongest words they had ever heard come out of the usually unflappable groom.

"I'm sorry," Christina answered. "She's probably tired of being cooped up. As soon as we get changed we'll turn them out for a while."

"We'll *try* to turn them out, you mean," Melanie said. "Star's getting a little too big to carry." Melanie had heard all about the time Mike and Christina had tried to take Star outside. But Christina hoped he

84

would be more confident with Nana beside him.

After Christina and Melanie changed into jeans and paddock boots, they headed back to the barn with their pockets stuffed with carrots.

"Just in case we have to lead Nana by her stomach again," Melanie joked.

Star dropped his small muzzle willingly through the leather noseband of the tiny halter. "Good boy," Christina said, bringing the strap over his head and buckling it into place. The colt leaned his head against her sweater, and Christina scratched him in his favorite place behind his ears. Star closed his eyes and grunted happily. Christina found herself imagining what it would be like to keep Star forever, to train and ride him herself, working with him every step of the way as he learned dressage and jumping. And one day . . . the Olympics!

"*Maaa*," Nana called, bringing Christina back to the present. The goat butted Christina's hip and looked up at her as if to hurry her along.

"Okay, okay," Christina said, snapping a cotton lead rope to the ring on Star's noseband. "I just have to practice leading Star around the stall a little."

Nana cocked her head sideways, then walked over and reared up against the door.

"Down," Melanie commanded from the aisle. "Shoo. I need to get in there."

As Melanie tried to convince Nana to back up so she could come in, Christina practiced leading Star around the stall. She kept one hand on the lead line, near his chin, and the other on his hindquarters so she could give a little push if he decided to stop. With her to guide him, the little foal walked forward willingly, and when Star had successfully circled the perimeter of his stall twice, Christina stopped him.

"Ready?" she asked Melanie, taking a deep breath. "Let's go."

Melanie clipped a lead line onto Nana's red leather collar. "I hope goats know how to heel," she joked.

When Melanie reached up to undo the latch, Nana pulled a carrot out of the back pocket of her jeans.

"Hey," Melanie said, spinning around. But Nana, with the stolen carrot dangling out of her mouth like an orange cigar, darted out the open door, dragging Melanie along behind her.

"Stop," Melanie called, but the big goat weighed nearly as much as she did, and Nana was in too much of a hurry to get outside. "Aren't there any brakes on this thing?" Melanie shouted over her shoulder as she was dragged right out the barn door.

Christina's laughter was cut short when she felt Star tense up beneath her hands. He whinnied anxiously for his friend, and before Christina could stop him, he bolted out of the stall. She had to use every bit of her strength to hold the colt to a walk as they scrambled down the aisle. Star's head turned like a periscope when he stepped into the March sunlight.

"It's okay. She's right over there," Christina said, leaning into his body to steer him to the right. Melanie was leading Nana into the paddock behind the barn. "Keep going," Christina called. "We're right behind you."

"Like I have a choice?" she heard her cousin yell back.

When Nana and Star were safely inside the paddock, the girls leaned against the fence to watch them. Christina felt as though a huge weight had been lifted from her shoulders. Star's head was high and he waved his scrappy tail like a flag as he pranced around Nana. It was hard to believe he was the same frightened little foal who, a few days ago, had pressed against the boards of his stall as though he were trying to become invisible.

"Something tells me that Nana is just what Star needed," Melanie said.

I hope she's right, Christina thought, smiling as she watched Star stretch his neck out to sniff the early spring grass.

They soon fell into an easy routine. Every morning Christina would brush Nana and Star, and lead them out into one of the grassy paddocks before she went to school. The broodmares all had tiny foals at their sides now, so it was best to keep the barn quiet during the day. When she got home in the afternoon, Christina would climb up on the fence and watch the colt romping and playing with the goat. While Christina still wasn't hacking Sterling or taking lessons at Whisperwood as often as she would have liked, seeing how Star had blossomed was well worth it.

Nana and Star made an odd-looking couple. The

leggy foal was already taller than his adopted mother, but there was no question about who was boss. When the colt kicked his heels up too close to the goat, Nana had only to lower her head and look in Star's direction and he would drop his eyes and wander a few yards away. Christina laughed as he spread his front legs wide like a giraffe, trying to reach the grass with his short neck. She had begun to supplement his Foal-Lac with milk pellets and weanling feed, and Star was growing bigger and stronger all the time.

One afternoon Christina heard Star whinnying as soon as she stepped off the school bus. She caught sight of the foal frantically trotting the fence line, his head held high and his nostrils flared as he called for Nana. But the goat was nowhere to be seen.

"Uh-oh," Christina muttered, running up the driveway without waiting for Melanie. She got to the paddock at the same time as Jonnie.

"Third time today that goat's jumped out," he said, trying to grab hold of Star's halter. The colt ducked away, trotting to the corner of the paddock before wheeling around and coming back toward them again. "Thinks she's queen of the mountain."

Christina followed his scowl and laughed when she saw Nana watching the commotion. The goat was perched high on top of the mounting block outside the paddock.

"I'll get her this time," she said, dropping her backpack on the ground.

Jonnie shrugged. "She'll just jump out again, now that she knows she can."

"*Maaa*." Nana jumped off the mounting block and met Christina halfway.

"You bad girl," Christina scolded, scratching the goat under her chin. "Shame on you for leaving Star by himself."

Nana followed Christina through the gate without a struggle, and Star trotted up to them, making a funny grumbling sound in his throat as he welcomed his friend.

"I don't know, Chris," Melanie called from the fence. "Star's starting to sound like a goat."

"He is not. He's just happy to be with his friend again. Aren't you, boy?" Christina crooned, stroking his neck. His coat was warm from the sun, and beneath the surface fuzz it glinted copper in the light. "Look," she said, pointing. "His coat's really starting to come in now. I was right—he's going to be exactly the same color as Wonder."

"And maybe he'll win the Kentucky Derby, too," Melanie said with a gleam in her eye. "Hey, I could be the winning jockey!"

Christina kept quiet as she watched Star scamper around Nana. She had already started thinking of Star as *her* horse. Why shouldn't she? Whitebrook had plenty of other foals to turn into racers, and no one else seemed to take much interest in Star, anyway. Christina couldn't buy out the Townsends' share of the colt, but maybe Brad Townsend would be willing to have Star trained as a three-day event horse, since he didn't think Star would ever amount to much. And if Christina and Star made it to the Olympics, both Townsend Acres and Whitebrook Farm could share in their glory.

"Here we go again," Melanie said.

Christina groaned as she saw a black-and-white flash out of the corner of her eye. She turned just in time to see Nana land nimbly in the grass on the outside of the paddock fence and trot over to the mounting block.

"She acts like it's her throne," Melanie observed.

Christina laughed. "I guess we have to find Her Highness something to stand on *inside* the fence so she'll stop getting out."

They found an old table in the attic, dragged it out to the paddock, and waited until Nana had climbed on top of the table and arranged herself with her front hooves dangling over the edge, looking settled and happy. By then Christina had only a little bit of the afternoon left to ride.

"I have to ride Sterling now," Christina said. "We have an event coming up in two weeks, and I don't even know my dressage test!"

"I'll bring Star and Nana in for you, Chris," Melanie offered.

"Thanks," Christina said gratefully as she headed into the barn. She made her way over to the tack room, grabbed a bucket of grooming tools, and led Sterling out into the aisle, where she put her in crossties.

"I'm sorry, girl," Christina said, quickly flicking the dirt off Sterling's black legs with a stiff dandy brush. "I promise I'll give you a bubble bath tomorrow." She tossed a quilted pad on Sterling's back before sliding the saddle into place behind her withers. As Christina reached under Sterling's barrel for the end of the girth, the mare stomped a front hoof impatiently.

"I know," Christina said, letting her hand rest on Sterling's dappled shoulder before fastening the girth. "You're probably fed up with my spending so much time with Star." Sterling wasn't exactly neglected, Christina thought. She just didn't have as much time to fuss over her mare the way she used to.

"I'll tell you what," she said, stopping to kiss Sterling's velvety muzzle before slipping off the halter. "After we practice our dressage test a little while, I'll take you out on the trails. Okay?"

Sterling stuck her nose in the air, flipping her upper lip back like a clown.

Christina laughed. "Was that a yes?"

They rode through their dressage test once, circling the back paddock over and over before Christina halted at the X and saluted the imaginary judge. Then she lengthened her reins and walked Sterling out onto the path to the fields. She just couldn't keep her mind focused on flat work that day.

"We've got to work harder if we're going to be ready for Stony Ridge," she said, leaning forward to brush a piece of straw out of Sterling's mane as they walked along. When she and Parker had filled out her entry form for the April event, it had still seemed far away. Now it was almost on top of them.

"From here on out," Christina said, gathering up her reins for a trot, "riding is going to be number one on my list. Tomorrow morning first thing, I'm going to drag the jumps out of the shed and get our course set up again so we don't have to hack over to Whisperwood to jump."

They skimmed across the spongy ground, with Sterling's front legs flicking far out ahead of her as though she were performing a lengthening across a dressage arena. As soon as Christina thought about increasing their pace, Sterling broke into a canter, almost as if their minds were linked. Christina pushed her heels deeper in the stirrups, locking her legs against Sterling's powerful sides as the warm wind whistled past her ears. This was where she belonged—at one with a galloping horse beneath her. And someday, she told herself, she'd be of one mind with Star.

10

With each passing day Star grew stronger and more confident. The colt no longer needed a bottle at all, and as the days grew longer, Christina could devote more time to riding Sterling.

The morning before the Stony Ridge event, Christina woke up with the birds, eager to begin the day. But when she rolled open the door to the mare and foal barn, she almost wished she had stayed in bed.

The concrete aisle had been neatly swept the night before, but it was now ankle deep in litter. Horse blankets, bandages, halters, and lead ropes were strewn everywhere, as though a tornado had pulled them off the pegs outside each stall, scrambling them in the air before moving on. And standing in the middle of the mess, ears pricked and eyes wide, were Nana and Star. *How did they get out?* Christina wondered worriedly.

"You two are so bad," she scolded. But even though she was angry, Christina was careful to keep her voice soft so Nana and Star wouldn't be afraid to let her catch them. When she rolled the door closed behind her and turned to walk toward them, her foot slid out from under her. She regained her balance and grimaced when she saw the torn horse calendar under her paddock boot. Either Star or Nana had managed to pull off all the papers that usually hung on the bulletin board outside the grain room. That meant there were push pins she'd have to find before someone's foot or hoof did. Good thing the grain room door was still locked. She shuddered to think of what she might have found if they had gone in there and overeaten.

Christina shut Star and Nana back in their stall and was examining the latch when she heard the door roll open behind her. She whipped her head around, relieved to see her cousin standing there instead of her mother or father.

Melanie whistled. "Nana did all this?"

Christina sighed. "With a little help from Star." The colt's head was turned sideways, his top lip wiggling as he tried to grab hold of the string on her hooded sweatshirt. Christina stepped back, taking his muzzle between her hands and giving him a quick kiss on his white star.

"Hurry, Mel, we've got to put these guys away and get this place picked up before Mom sees it," she said, slipping Star's halter on. Before Wonder died, her mother would have laughed at something like this, but now Christina wasn't so sure.

"We?" Melanie raised her eyebrows skeptically.

"I'll owe you one," Christina promised, bending down to scoop up some halters.

When they had gotten everything off the floor and were rolling up the last of the bandages, Christina heard a click. She looked up just as Nana finished wiggling the stall door latch open with her nose.

"Oh, no, you don't," she said, lunging for the door before Nana had even gotten her front hooves back on the ground again. *So that's how they got out,* she mused. She knew her parents had to screw big metal rings under the latches in the stalls of horses who had learned how to escape. When an old lead line clasp was fastened on the ring, a horse couldn't wiggle the handle of the latch up and slide the bolt open.

Christina found one of the rings and screwed it into the wood. She clipped a lead line clasp onto the ring and stood back. Nana shook her head and jumped up on the door, nibbling at the latch, but it stayed put. The goat was certainly proving to be a lot of trouble, but Star was doing so well that Christina knew she'd have to put up with Nana's tricks for a while longer.

"Hold still, will you?" Christina said, standing on a stool in the barn aisle as she tried to keep hold of Sterling's slippery mane. She knew she shouldn't have shampooed her mane when she gave Sterling a bath—clean hair was a lot harder to braid than dirty hair—but Christina had wanted Sterling to look especially nice for her first event of the season. She glanced at her watch. If she didn't hurry and finish up, it would be time for Jonnie to feed the horses, and then it would be impossible to make Sterling stand still.

As she divided the next section of mane into three parts, Christina ran through the dressage test in her head. *Working trot down center line, circle right ten meters, leg yield left from D to H.* She was so busy concentrating that she practically fell off the stool when the barn door opened in front of them.

"You're up bright and early," Jonnie said. "When are your times?"

"Eleven-twenty-seven for dressage, and one-thirty for cross-country. Parker's going to pick us up in an hour so we can get there and have time to look around."

"Hey, you. Get down from there," Jonnie said, waving his hands in front of Star's door. Christina laughed as the two heads disappeared back into the stall. Star had learned to brace his front hooves against the door, the way Nana did, when something interesting was going on in the aisle.

"First time I've ever seen a horse that thinks he's a goat," Jonnie said, shaking his head.

With motherly pride, Christina watched Star and Nana playfully butting each other around the stall. A month earlier, Christina never would have left Star to

96

ride in an event. But the timid and fearful colt that Star had once been was now gone. And with Nana at his side, the colt seemed perfectly content to be left alone. *Maybe in a few years I'll have Star in crossties as I braid his mane for an important event,* she thought with a smile.

"Hey, gorgeous," Melanie said, bringing Christina out of her daydream.

"Thanks," Christina answered, batting her eyelashes.

Her cousin squinted up at her. "I was talking about *Sterling.* You, on the other hand . . . "

Christina hooked her thumbs into the straps of the overalls she always wore to braid. The bib had just the right number of pockets for the comb, rubber bands, scissors, and tape. "You're just jealous because you don't know how to dress like a country girl."

"And I hope I never learn." Melanie let Sterling lick her hand. "I wish your event were tomorrow so you could come to the races with us today. It's more fun when you're there, too," she said wistfully.

Christina hadn't been to the racetrack in ages. It seemed as though every time her parents asked, Chris had something else to do. "Are any of our horses going to run next weekend?" Christina asked. "Maybe I could go then."

Melanie grinned. "Well, Ashleigh wants to try Missy in a maiden race in May. You could come and see how your prodigy runs."

"Great," Christina said, groaning. "She'll probably

still be shying at the grandstand when everyone else is crossing the finish line."

"We'll see," Melanie said with a laugh. "Good luck at the event!"

On the way to Stony Ridge, Christina rubbed her palms against her knees.

"Nervous?" Parker took his eyes off the road a second and smiled at her.

"Excited," Christina said. "I can't wait to go cross-country." It was her favorite part of an event: galloping like the wind over a mile-and-a-half-long course with twenty-two jumps.

"I hope your first cross-country run this season will be better than mine was," Parker said.

Christina had heard all about how Foxy bobbled, going down on one knee as she landed after the splash jump and rocketing Parker over her head into the water. Foxy was about as surefooted as they came, but cross-country, like racing, didn't leave room for any false steps.

When they turned into the driveway of Stony Ridge, Christina saw the usual chaotic scene. Unlike shows and races, where the action took place in a ring or on a track and all the spectators gathered in one place to watch, events had more the look of a market day, with horses and riders going in all directions.

Three rectangular arenas with low white fences

were off to the left. The horses and riders who congregated there were dressed as though they were going to a fancy ball: horses with flowing tails and manes that marched in small, even plaits down their elegant necks, riders whose snowy white breeches peeked out from under tailored black hunt coats or shadbelly coats with long tails.

The picture to the right of the driveway was more colorful. Cross-country riders with shirts and hat covers as bright as racing silks sat astride horses with nostrils flaring and legs encased in matching bandages and jumping boots. Later all would return to formal black coats to ride in stadium jumping, the third phase of the event.

"I'll get our number packets while you park," Christina said, opening the truck door when Parker stopped to let some riders pass. As she headed for the registration desk she walked slowly so that she could watch a rider steer a big black horse into the starting box for cross-country. There was something familiar about the pair.

The horse wheeled around and burst from the box in a bounding canter, eager to be off and running. Christina recognized the rider, sitting cool and collected on top of the dynamo. Christina could tell that she was quietly pacing her horse so that he would jump the first fence at a safe distance.

It was Eliza and Flash, all right. Christina had met the older girl at an event camp two summers before. It had been over a year since she'd last seen Eliza, but Christina knew her friend must be doing well to be competing in the advanced division, two levels higher than Christina and Parker.

Christina felt a shiver of excitement as she watched Eliza and Flash jump the second fence and disappear into the woods. As soon as she and Sterling were done with their dressage test, they'd be flying, too.

When Sterling entered the dressage arena, trotting down the center line and halting at the X, Christina knew it was going to be a good test. She could feel the extra spring in Sterling's stride as they moved from halt to trot in one fluid movement. It was as though the mare liked being in the spotlight, performing intricate patterns in front of the group of hushed spectators. When Christina dropped her head and white-gloved hand in a final salute at the end of the test, her heart was pounding with exhilaration.

"Nice test, stranger," a voice called as Christina rode Sterling out of the arena on a loose rein.

Christina turned her head. "Eliza!"

"Sterling looks awesome," Eliza said enthusiastically, flipping her thick braid over one shoulder.

"Thanks," Christina answered, the older girl's praise suddenly making her feel shy. "Did you and Flash go clean in cross-country?"

"No time faults, even. He was great." Eliza patted the black horse's sweaty neck.

"So what have you guys been up to?" Christina

asked, swinging her leg over Sterling's back and sliding to the ground. "Have you tried out for the Young Riders team yet?"

"The selection trials are later this summer," Eliza said with a worried frown. "I'm exercising horses at the track and saving up so we can go."

Christina was surprised. "Exercising racehorses?"

"Yup. The money's good, and it's really taught me how to rate a horse. I think that's what's helping me get Flash around cross-country without any time faults this year." The tall girl smiled. "Anyway, I'd better keep cooling him off."

"Good luck," Christina called as Eliza clucked Flash forward.

"You too. And watch the footing after the water jump. The ground's a little soft," Eliza added. "Catch you later!"

On the way back to the trailer, Christina thought about what Eliza had said about exercising racehorses.

"Did you learn a lot riding racehorses?" she asked Parker as he squatted down to fasten galloping boots on Foxy's legs.

Parker glanced over his shoulder at her. "Things getting a little slow around here for you?"

"No," Christina said. "I just wondered if maybe I should start helping out with the exercising at White-brook. It might give us a boost in cross-country."

"Couldn't hurt. The exercise riding I did in England definitely helped me develop my uncanny sense of balance," Parker joked, wiggling his eyebrows comically.

"Well, I hope your uncanny sense of balance keeps you a little drier today," Christina said.

"Ten, nine, eight . . ."

Christina and Sterling were standing in the starting box for the cross-country course with their backs to the opening so Sterling wouldn't leap out too soon and be disqualified. Christina flexed her fingers on the rubber-coated reins, bending Sterling around her right leg.

When the starter gave them the go-ahead, Sterling was pointed toward the first fence. Christina pushed the big stopwatch button on her watch as she closed her legs against her mare's sides. They were off!

Christina couldn't hear anything but the pounding of hooves and the air whistling past her ears as Sterling carried her to the first fence—a solid chicken coop. She kept her hands quiet against the Thoroughbred's neck, straightening in the saddle as Sterling shifted her weight back in preparation for takeoff. Three strides, two strides, one stride, then Sterling gathered her legs together and soared over the coop with a foot to spare.

"Good girl," Christina said as they continued on. Sterling galloped across the field, hesitating only briefly before leaping across a wide ditch lined with boards— the coffin jump. Christina didn't know which felt better, soaring over the huge fences or landing and galloping on, Sterling's hooves digging into the grass as they flew past spectators and fence judges. She loved the even rhythm of Sterling's breath, matching each stride as they sailed over stone walls, water jumps, and sharp drops.

She wasn't sure when the change happened, but after Sterling jumped the fourteenth fence—the hay wagon—Christina had to really push the mare on as they galloped up the hill. Usually Sterling leaned against the bit, eagerly galloping up to the next fence. But the mare's pace was definitely flagging.

Christina sat back in the saddle as she assessed the situation. The mare's strides were even, so she wasn't lame. *She's getting tired*, Christina realized as Sterling put in an extra stride before jumping the cordwood fence. She couldn't remember Sterling ever running out of energy before, but she knew why it was happening that day. Christina had been spending so much time with Star, she hadn't been working Sterling enough. And now she was pushing the mare too hard.

"Okay, girl. Let's take the rest slow and easy," Christina said, easing Sterling down to a trot. She knew that tired horses were more apt to make mistakes, such as catching their hooves on jumps or taking off at the wrong time and falling. Christina didn't want to take any chances.

By the time they approached the last jump, a group of whiskey barrels standing upright in a solid row, Christina was pushing Sterling every step of the way.

"One more, girl. You can do it."

The mare's ears flicked back and forth as she cleared

the barrels and, with a sudden burst of speed, swept between the finish flags.

Christina swung out of the saddle before Sterling had even dropped to a walk. She tossed the reins over Sterling's head and threw the stirrup irons over the saddle, loosening the girth two holes. Sterling's coat was almost black with sweat, and her nostrils flared pink as she puffed tiredly.

"Good girl," Christina said over and over as she walked Sterling around the edge of the warm-up field. Sterling had given her all; Christina only hoped that she hadn't asked the mare for too much. The mare's sides were still heaving, and as Christina walked her slowly around to cool off, she decided she would have to scratch Sterling from stadium jumping. It just wasn't worth the risk. Besides, she was anxious to get home and see how Star was doing.

"One down, three to go," Parker said as they drove home from the event. Since both Sterling and Foxy had gone clean in cross-country, they were on their way toward earning the four clear rounds they needed to qualify to compete in three-day events.

When Christina didn't say anything, Parker gave her a little punch on the arm. "You're not upset about missing stadium, are you?"

"No," Christina said, slumping in her seat. "I'm worried about Sterling, that's all."

"She was just tired from cross-country," Parker said. "Next time you'll pace her better."

Christina looked at Parker's red second-place ribbon hanging from the rearview mirror. Sterling might have placed, too, if Christina had rated her differently during cross-country. She thought about her conversation with Eliza once more. *Maybe I should try exercise riding*, she thought.

After Christina had made Sterling a warm bran mash and put her away for the night, she went to check on Star. The colt was lying down, eyes closed, nose resting lightly on Nana's back. The goat had her feet tucked under her and was quietly chewing her cud. Christina decided not to disturb them, and lugged her eventing gear up to the house.

She heard the laughter as soon as she opened the mud room door. Ashleigh, Samantha, Melanie, and Naomi were sitting around the kitchen table.

"Good day at the track?" Christina asked, dropping her stuff in a pile by the pantry.

"Wind Chaser won," Samantha said, her face glowing with pride over the Secretariat colt she owned jointly with her father, Ian.

"And Misty Princess beat a whole field of colts!" Naomi exclaimed.

Christina smiled at the young jockey. "So you had two wins?"

"Three," Naomi said. "I rode another trainer's colt, too."

"Wow. Congratulations," Christina said, grabbing a tortilla chip and leaning over the end of the table to reach the dip.

"How was your event?" her mother asked.

Christina managed a small smile back. "Okay, I guess. Sterling was second after dressage and she went clean in cross-country, but she was so tired I decided to scratch from stadium."

Ashleigh put her hand on Christina's arm. "That doesn't sound too bad for your first time out this year."

Christina shrugged.

"How come you look so bummed out?" Melanie asked, getting to the point in her usual frank way.

"I don't know. I think I pushed her too fast in cross-country." She turned to her mother. "Do you think I could start exercise-riding some of the racehorses?"

Ashleigh eyes widened in surprise. "Of course you can. Your dad and I would love to have your help."

Christina grabbed a handful of chips and leaned against the counter. "I think it might help me learn how to pace her better," she explained.

Samantha nodded. "I would have suggested it before, but you always seemed so determined to stay away from racing."

Christina glanced at Ashleigh, but her mother was tracing designs in the moisture on the outside of her glass. "It's not that I don't like racing," Christina explained. "It's just that I think eventing is a lot more exciting."

Melanie and Naomi shook their heads as though she were out of her mind, and her mother didn't say anything. Only Samantha nodded in understanding.

"Well, I guess I'll go jump in the shower," Christina said, suddenly feeling out of place.

Christina hadn't even reached the stairs before they began to rehash the races once more. Maybe if she did a little exercise-riding, she might feel more like she belonged.

11

WHEN CHRISTINA AND MELANIE GOT OFF THE BUS ON Monday afternoon, Christina was looking forward to her first exercise-riding lesson with her mother. But when she went out to the paddock to bring in Nana and Star, they were gone. Anxiously she rushed into the barn.

"At least it will grow back," Ashleigh was saying to Mike as Christina burst into the barn. Her parents turned, waiting for her to come down the aisle.

"What's the matter?" she asked worriedly when she saw their unsmiling faces. "Is Star all right?"

"That goat of yours ate Perfect Heart's tail," Mike said, his face stern.

Christina was so relieved that Star wasn't injured, she laughed out loud. But her parents weren't amused.

"She chewed the hair off almost to the tailbone," her

mother added, her frown deepening. "How can we turn her out during fly season without a tail?"

"Maybe I could braid some hair extensions on?" Christina suggested, trying to keep a straight face.

"This is not a joke, Christina," Mike said, his usually cheerful voice stern. "What if it had been one of the mares in for breeding? Can you imagine us trying to explain to the owner that a goat had ruined his valuable broodmare's tail?"

"But how do you know Nana did it?" Christina pointed out. "Couldn't she have gotten it caught in the fence?"

Ashleigh shook her head impatiently. "Heart was in the next paddock over. I caught that goat red-handed, but it was too late. Heart's tail is as scrawny as an Appaloosa's now."

"I'm sorry," Christina said. "Maybe if I give her more hay next time—"

"There isn't going to be a next time," her mother interrupted, shaking her head.

Christina felt her heartbeat quicken with alarm. "What do you mean?"

Mike put his arm around Ashleigh's shoulders, as if to demonstrate to Christina that they had settled the matter together already. "This is a Thoroughbred farm, not a petting zoo," he said. "And Star is old enough to be on his own. It's time to send the goat back."

Christina saw that there was no changing their minds. "I'll call Mrs. Devon," she said quietly.

As soon as she got off the phone with Nana's owner, Christina called Parker to arrange for him to pick her up. Christina decided to stay with Star while Kevin and Parker took Nana back to Mrs. Devon's. Christina wasn't sure how Star was going to react, but she knew Nana wouldn't go without a fuss. Exercise riding would have to wait until another day—Star needed her now.

"All right," Parker said when he pulled up in front of the barn. "One farewell kiss, and then it's bye-bye, goat." He jumped down from his truck and followed Christina into the barn.

"I'm going to miss you, you little rascal," Christina said, kneeling down in the stall to take Nana's face between her hands. Christina could smell onion grass on the goat's breath.

"*Maaa*," Nana bleated as she pulled away, her tail wagging like a dog's.

"Okay. One last carrot." Christina reached around for the one she had hidden in her back pocket.

"Come on. We have to get going so I can get back in time to ride Foxy." Parker ran his finger over his upper lip. He'd been doing that a lot since he started to shave. "You could take Sterling out with us."

Christina bit her lip. "I'd better see how Star is after Nana leaves." She was worried the colt would act the same way foals did when they were weaned from their mothers—frantic and scared. She couldn't leave him until she was sure Star wouldn't hurt himself.

Parker nodded. "But remember, we have only two

more weeks until the Spring Run horse trials."

"Parker, you coming?" Kevin called, sticking his head into the barn. "I've got the tarp spread."

"Tarp?" Christina raised her eyebrows.

Parker blushed. "You know, in case she, uh . . . goes to the bathroom again." He gave the lead line a tug. "Come on, goat."

Nana went through the door willingly, eager to get out to graze. Star lunged for the door to follow her.

"No, you have to stay inside a little while," Christina said, grasping his halter firmly.

"Good luck," Kevin said as he latched the stall door. "And be careful."

Star's whole body shook as he whinnied desperately for his friend. When the colt stopped to take a breath, Christina could hear Nana's plaintive answer over the sound of the truck's engine as it disappeared down the driveway.

Christina thought her heart would break as she felt Star tremble. "It's okay," she said, trying to soothe the colt. "I'm still here."

But Star's eyes were wild. He reared up, tearing his halter out of her grasp, and Christina was suddenly afraid. It was all she could do to slip out the door before Star tried to ram his way through the opening. She hated having to yell and swing the lead line in front of him, but it was the only way to keep him away.

Once she was out of the stall, Star reared up again, planting his front hooves against the door.

"No," Christina shouted, waving her arms. She was afraid he would try to jump out and injure himself. Star backed away, his screams as shrill as a stallion's calling for a mare.

The colt cantered in circles around the stall, his frantic cries tearing at her heart. There was no way Christina could leave him now. When Star finally slowed to a walk and then stopped altogether, his sides heaving and his coat wet with sweat, Christina felt broken, too.

First Wonder, now Nana, Christina thought. *How much more unhappiness can Star take?*

She unlatched the door and went inside again, burying her face in the colt's soft mane. Star nuzzled her chest, blowing out soft, warm breaths. Christina rubbed his ears, talking softly to him. "It's all right, boy. I'm here. I won't leave you."

Later Christina sneaked out to the barn to spend the night in Star's stall. The colt slept fitfully, jumping up from the straw and whinnying at the door at every sound. By morning Star seemed to have given up on Nana, but he stuck to Christina like a shadow, even trying to slip out the door with her when she left to get his grain. She had only made it halfway down the aisle when his anxious whinnying began once more. Christina sat with him while he ate his breakfast, wondering what she should do. It was a school day, but how could she leave Star alone when he was so miserable?

An hour before the school bus was due, Christina hurried into the stallion barn to find her parents. Ashleigh was measuring out grain into a row of green plastic buckets.

"Can I miss school today, Mom?" Christina asked her mother's bent back. "I have to sit with Star. He's really upset."

But Ashleigh didn't respond. She just kept measuring out quarts of sweet feed, bran, and oats.

"Mom?" Christina demanded. "Did you hear what I said?"

Ashleigh tossed the quart measure into the feed bin and closed the lid. "Yes," she answered, picking the buckets up by the handles. "And no, you may not skip school. I don't want your grades dropping because of that colt."

Her mother's tone was icy—the same tone she always used when Christina wanted to discuss Star. Was Christina imagining things, or did her mother really not like the little colt?

"But someone has to watch Star," Christina said desperately, following her mother as she made her way down the aisle with the buckets.

"I'll watch him for you, Chris."

It was Mike, standing in the doorway of the tack room.

Christina looked up at him gratefully. "Thanks,

Dad," she said. "Star's really taking this badly."

"Don't worry," Mike assured her. "We'll come up with something."

When Christina came back from school that afternoon, she raced into the barn, dropping her bag in the aisle as she ran to Star's stall. But the door hung open—Star wasn't there.

Through the open barn door, Christina caught sight of her father, leaning on the fence to the smallest paddock near the barn. When she got there, Christina saw that he had turned Star out with Silver Jane and her gray filly, Catwink. But Star was hovering in the corner, and Mike didn't look happy.

"He called for you for two hours after you left," Mike explained. "I thought he'd like the company, but he's really testing that mare's patience."

Christina watched Star, a lump rising in her throat. The colt had seen her and whinnied for her, but Silver Jane and Catwink were blocking Star's path to where Christina stood by the fence. Star reared up on his hind legs, coming down with his head lowered—just like a goat—ready to butt Catwink out of the way. Silver Jane lunged out at him, gnashing her teeth, and scared the colt back into the corner.

"He can't go on acting like this, Chris," Mike went on. "He's got to learn that he's a *horse*, and start behaving like one."

• • •

"I know, Dad," Christina muttered, though she wasn't sure Star would ever learn.

"Let's put him away for now," Mike said.

Christina grabbed a lead rope and walked out to where Star was waiting for her in the corner. He nickered happily when he saw her approach, and tears sprang into Christina's eyes. How could the colt be so wonderful and cause so much trouble and pain at the same time? She rubbed his forehead, and he nudged her hand gently in response. *I just have find a way to keep Star happy,* Christina thought as she led the colt back into the barn.

The following afternoon Christina and Melanie decided to turn Star out alone. After all, it was horses that he didn't get along with, not people. As long as she was there with him, Christina was sure he'd be okay.

While they were sitting on the fence watching Star, Christina tried to remember the last time she had just hung out with her cousin. *Not since Star was born,* Christina thought.

"I bet we could teach him to fetch," Melanie said. Star had the end of a lead rope in his mouth and was playing tug-of-war with Melanie. The colt yanked so hard on the rope, he almost pulled her off the fence.

"Stop treating him like a dog," Christina scolded. "You'll give him an identity problem."

"He already has an identity problem," Melanie said, laughing as Star trotted away with the rope dangling from his teeth. Then he whirled around and trotted back. But instead of stopping in front of the fence, he reared up as though he was going to put his hooves in Melanie's lap.

"Watch it," Christina yelled, rolling off the fence. Melanie fell in a heap beside her.

Star veered away, cantering around the paddock and bucking like a bronc.

"Are you okay?" Christina said, kneeling by her cousin.

"I think so," Melanie said, sounding shaken. She got slowly to her feet. "He's too big for that kind of stuff, though."

"He's just feeling good," Christina said defensively. But she knew her cousin was right. And it would only get worse. Unless Star began spending time with other horses, he was going to become more and more dangerous the bigger he grew.

Her parents were meeting with clients in the stallion barn when it was time to turn out the broodmares the next morning. Christina decided it was just as well, since she wasn't sure how Star would react to her latest plan. She waited until Jonnie had led a pair of mares and their foals far out into the front pasture before hurrying into the aisle.

"I'm going to turn you and Raven out in the paddock," she explained to Perfect Heart as she led the mare down the aisle. She didn't have to worry about leading Raven, the mare's pretty black filly, who pranced by her mother's hindquarters as though she were tied with an invisible thread. Christina had chosen them because Perfect Heart was so docile and sweet—sweet enough to let a goat eat her tail! Christina couldn't imagine Perfect Heart hurting Star. Just because Star hadn't gotten along with one mare and her foal didn't mean he couldn't make friends with another.

When she went back in the barn for Star, Melanie was waiting in the stall. "It's one thing if your parents get mad at *you*," her cousin said. "The worst that could happen is that you'd get grounded or something. But what about me? I don't want them to send me back to New York."

"Don't be such a worrywart. Nothing's going to happen," Christina said. "Besides missing the bus if we don't hurry," she added.

They led Star out to the paddock without anyone stopping to ask what they were doing. So far, so good.

Christina walked the colt out into the middle of the paddock and unclipped his lead rope.

"Go ahead, Star," Christina told him. "Play with Raven." She waved her arms in the air, but Star stood as still as a Breyer model, staring at Perfect Heart and Raven as though he'd never seen horses before. He was like a little kid on his first day at school.

"You silly boy," Christina said, reaching up to pat

117

his taut neck. "Just be yourself—I'm sure you'll get along fine."

Perfect Heart was already grazing contentedly, but her little black filly was feeling rambunctious. Raven took a few steps toward Star, her nose quivering. Star held his ground, and Christina backed away to the fence to watch.

Raven took two more steps toward Star, and the colt stretched out his neck. Their muzzles were almost touching.

All of a sudden Raven bolted away, her long legs scrambling as she circled the grassy paddock.

Star came out of his trance. With a squeal, he took off after the filly, his tail raised as he galloped in pursuit.

Were they going to fight? Christina's heart was in her throat as she watched Star slide to a stop in front of the filly.

And then he took off again, this time with Raven in his wake. They raced through the grass, swerving around Perfect Heart and galloping past Christina and Melanie as if they weren't even there.

"They're playing tag," Melanie said.

Christina's heart slid back where it belonged, filling her chest.

Star had made his first horse friend.

That afternoon Christina found her father leaning against the paddock fence, watching Star and Raven play. Beyond the paddocks, Ashleigh was leading Pride's Perfection in from the pasture.

"They are having way too much fun," Mike said, smiling when he saw Christina. "I decided to leave them out all day."

Christina stood next to her father and watched as Star nibbled at Raven's withers. The little filly's eyes were closed, and she bobbed her head happily while her new friend scratched the hard-to-reach spot.

"Hey, boy," Christina called out to the colt. But Star was too busy with Raven to respond. He must have nibbled a bit too hard, because suddenly Raven squealed and half reared, then took off in a dead run the moment her hooves touched the ground. The filly raced to the other end of the paddock, Star hot on her heels. They didn't stop at the fence, but galloped around the perimeter of the paddock as if it were a racetrack.

Just then Ashleigh came walking along the paddock fence, leading Pride's Perfection into the wash stall outside the racing barn. She didn't even glance their way. But when Star galloped by, Ashleigh stopped and stared, her face as white as a ghost's.

Maybe now Mom will see how wonderful Star is, Christina wished hopefully. But Ashleigh kept on staring silently at the colt as he galloped by.

Soon Star had caught up with the filly, and side by side they raced past Christina and Mike. Star's coat shone like copper in the bright sun as he outran Raven, slowing to a trot once he had passed her.

"That's some colt," Mike breathed.

Christina stared at her father incredulously.

"I mean it, Chris," Mike said earnestly. "He's really something. And he's looking more like Wonder every day. If he keeps this up, we might just have a champion on our hands."

Tears welled up in Christina's eyes, and she had to turn her head away. She wasn't sure if he knew it, but her father's words meant the world to her. If only she could hear her mother say the same thing about Star. But Ashleigh turned her back as she led Pride's Perfection off to the wash stall.

"So he can go out with Raven every day, then," Melanie said, poking her head into the bathroom as Christina was getting ready for bed. "Your problems are solved."

"I guess," Christina said, spitting toothpaste into the sink. She wasn't sure why, but she didn't feel as happy about Star's breakthrough as she should have.

"Fine. Everybody's so touchy around here," Melanie muttered as she slunk away. "Good night, Grumpy."

"Good night," Christina called after her.

Melanie's right, Christina thought as she went back to her room. *Ever since Wonder died people* have *been acting different. Especially Mom.* But Christina didn't know what she could do to make things better.

12

"IT'S FUN SEEING SOMEONE ELSE GET TORTURED BY OLD HAY Bales for a change," Melanie said the following Saturday.

Christina groaned as she settled back in the small racing saddle that was propped on top of two hay bales—her "horse" for the first week of her training as an exercise rider. The muscles in her legs were quivering from trying to stand up in the short, jockey-length stirrups. But if she was going to ride racehorses, she was determined to do it right.

"Maybe Ashleigh will put you up on Missy," Melanie said with a wicked gleam in her eye.

"Only if I can have my own saddle back," Christina said. "No way could I stay on Missy in this tiny thing."

"You'll get used to it, Chris," Melanie said, laughing

as she walked down the aisle. "It'll get easier once they put you up on a real horse."

Christina grabbed at the hay bales, almost losing her balance once more. "I hope so," she muttered.

"Getting the hang of it?" Parker called from where he had been watching her in the aisle.

Christina looked up and blushed. *I must look like an idiot, crouched over a bale of hay.*

"I've had better rides," she joked, adjusting her seat.

"He looks like a handful," Parker commented, eyeing the hay bales.

Christina laughed, nearly toppling off as she lost her balance once more. Parker rushed forward, catching her by the elbow. Christina grabbed his shoulder to steady herself and dismounted awkwardly.

"I think that's enough for one day," she said, feeling embarrassed. "Ready to go on a real ride?"

"Foxy's waiting," Parker said, pointing to where his pretty bay mare was standing in the crossties.

"Sterling's all set to go," Christina said. "I just want to check on Star."

Parker followed her outside to where the colt was grazing in the paddock with Raven and Perfect Heart.

Star was doing better each day now that he had horses to learn from and play with. The colt and Raven were best friends, and each morning Star stood at his stall door, nickering eagerly for Christina to take him out to the paddock. Star had completely shed his baby fur, and his copper coat shone from hours spent in the warm sun.

"He's looking more like Wonder every day," Parker commented. "I can't wait for my granddad to see him."

Christina didn't answer, but she knew what Parker meant. Clay Townsend had always kept a special place in his heart for Wonder and her foals. She knew he'd be impressed when he saw Star.

The chestnut colt looked so peaceful and happy, Christina knew she had nothing to worry about. From now on Star was going to be all right.

Now that she needed to spend less time looking after Star, Christina was able to ride Sterling more often, and after a week of practicing on Old Hay Bales, she was ready to learn to exercise-ride, too.

"I want to start you out on Pride's Perfection," Ashleigh said when Christina walked into the racing barn early that Saturday.

"Do you think I'm ready?" Christina asked nervously. She wasn't sure she was ready to graduate from the hay bales to a horse.

Ashleigh smiled encouragingly. "Of course you're ready. If it had been up to me, I'd have been using you years ago."

Christina frowned and turned toward Perfection's stall. She couldn't help but take Ashleigh's comment as a jab at her for never showing any interest in racing.

But it was nice to see her mother so cheerful again. Christina only hoped Ashleigh wouldn't be disappointed when she saw her ride.

She led the five-year-old gelding out of his stall to groom him and tack him up. Christina was grateful she didn't have to start off on an unpredictable two-year-old such as Missy. Perfection was in his third season of racing and had excellent manners under saddle.

Christina was still brushing Perfection's chestnut coat to a deep orange sheen when Melanie walked out into the aisle leading Missy, all tacked up and ready to go.

"We'll meet you out there, unless you're going to braid him, too," Melanie teased.

Christina playfully stuck out her tongue at her cousin before turning back to Perfection. *Why am I stalling?* she asked herself. But she knew why. She'd shunned horse racing for years—what if she wasn't good enough to do the job?

Perfection sniffed the brush in her hand and shook his head impatiently.

"You ready to go, boy?" She reached for the exercise saddle that she'd placed on the floor near the crossties. It was so small and light, Christina wondered what it was going to feel like, galloping a horse with so little between her and his back.

When Christina finally led Perfection down to the training oval, she could see Melanie jogging Missy back toward the gate. Missy's nostrils were flared, and the veins stood out along her neck and stomach from the workout.

"She felt good out there," Melanie called to Ashleigh. "How was her time?"

"Not bad," Ashleigh answered. "A furlong in ten and change."

Melanie's eyes widened. "An eighth of a mile in just over ten seconds? If she keeps this up, I bet she'll win on Saturday!"

Ashleigh shrugged. "With a filly like this, you never know how she'll act the first time she races." She smiled at Christina. "You ready for a leg up?" she asked brightly.

Mom really loves this, Christina observed silently. "As ready as I'll ever be," she said, trying to ignore the nervous quiver in her stomach.

She put her knee into Ashleigh's cupped hands and was boosted up into the saddle. The next thing she knew, she was perched on top of Perfection. "Whoa," she said, automatically checking the colt as he stepped to one side.

Ashleigh stuck Christina's left paddock boot into the stirrup, checking for length. "This is a little on the long side, but it'll do. No point in jacking the leathers up too much your first time out."

"These are *long*?" Christina said in awe. Her legs were already beginning to ache. "They feel about four inches shorter than cross-country length!"

"Well, the horse has enough to do running a race.

He doesn't need a rider's legs banging his sides." Ashleigh tilted her head. "Perfection is just coming back from a race, so we only want to stretch his legs a bit, to limber him up."

Christina nodded, trying to ignore how sweaty her hands felt on the reins.

"Trot him around the track clockwise. You don't want him to think he's going to run this morning. Then, if he feels okay, let him move up to a canter. Got it?"

"Got it," Christina answered. But when she closed her legs to get Perfection moving in a walk, she felt as though she were four again, when her mother used to put her up on Wonder's back and lead her around. Her stirrups were too short for her legs to be useful, and she had to resist clutching at the pommel of the saddle to stay on. Instead, she concentrated on keeping her weight centered and her eyes up.

When Perfection reached the middle of the track, he swung his head around to look at Christina, as if to ask, *What next?* Christina let out her breath. It was now or never.

Not trusting her legs, she clucked, and Perfection responded with a buoyant trot that sent Christina bouncing high above the saddle. She remembered what it felt like to be a beginning rider, desperately trying to find her balance at the trot. The slightest movement of her feet sent her falling forward or back in the saddle, until she finally leaned forward on Perfection's withers and grabbed a piece of mane to help steady herself.

126

Perfection's ears flicked back and forth, but he kept his long-legged rhythm steady, and by the time they reached the first turn, Christina was beginning to get the hang of it.

She shortened her reins, pushing her hands further up Perfection's neck. That way she could balance over her knees. Her leg muscles were overtired from posting, so Christina tried staying up off his back, almost as if she were going over a jump.

Perfection took her change of position as a signal to canter. He leaped forward eagerly until Christina sat back, bringing him down to a trot once more. When they had completed one circuit, Ashleigh shouted out, "Let him canter now. But keep it slow."

"Okay, boy," Christina urged, easing her hands forward again. Instantly Perfection broke into a canter, his enormous stride eating up the track.

Christina had seen enough races and pictures of Ashleigh racing Wonder to know what a professional jockey's position looked like: back arched forward, chest low, arms way out in front of her. She imitated the position as best she could, and Perfection's stride lengthened until he seemed to be gliding along, barely skimming the ground. Christina followed the rhythm of his canter, maintaining a steady give-and-take on the reins. By the time she passed her mother again, she and Perfection were moving as one—and it felt fantastic!

"That's enough for today, Chris," Ashleigh called. "Bring him back slowly."

Christina was tempted to pretend she didn't hear her mother's voice behind her. She wanted to let Perfection gallop, to feel him stretch out until he was running like the wind.

But not today. Not ever, if she didn't follow instructions. Christina sighed as she lowered her seat into the saddle and brought Perfection back to a trot and then a walk.

The saddle didn't feel nearly as strange now, but the muscles in her legs were aching. "Good boy," Christina said, leaning forward to pat Perfection's warm chestnut neck as they circled back to the gate. Mike was standing next to Ashleigh now, and Christina could see that both her parents were beaming happily.

"That was beautiful, Chris!" Ashleigh called out. "How'd it feel?"

"Great!" Christina responded honestly.

"Well, you look like a real pro," Mike enthused. "There may be a future in racing for you after all, huh?"

Christina halted in front of them and toyed with Perfection's mane. "Well, I didn't say that . . . ," she started. Why couldn't her parents just accept the fact that she preferred eventing to racing? Their smiles began to fade. "But it was fun," she added hastily. "And I think it really will help me in cross-country."

Mike stepped forward to take Perfection's head so Christina could dismount. "Maybe one day we'll see you up there on Star," her father said as she swung down from the big colt's back.

"Yeah," Christina said. "But it will be in the Olympics, not on the track," she pointed out.

"If he's ever rideable," Ashleigh said, her face suddenly stony. She turned away before Christina had a chance to answer.

Christina watched her mother's retreating back. *So it isn't my imagination,* she thought, thunderstruck. *Mom really doesn't like Star.*

Christina felt uneasy at the thought. It was so unlike her mother to act that way toward any horse, especially Wonder's own foal. What had Star done that was so awful? As far as Christina could tell, he was the most wonderful colt in the world. *Someday soon Star will win Mom over,* Christina hoped. If only Ashleigh would give him a chance.

By May Christina was exercising as many horses as Melanie. She was counting the days when school would be out so she'd have more time to spend with Star and Sterling.

On the morning of the Kentucky Derby, Christina and Melanie woke up early, as usual, and headed out to the racing barn.

"Maybe Parker will forget," Melanie said, yawning sleepily.

"I doubt it. He thought it was the best idea he'd ever had," Christina laughed.

Parker's idea was to turn Christina and Melanie's

morning exercise ride on the day of the Derby into a match race. He'd instructed them to wear racing silks and put numbers on their horses' saddle pads— Christina was number one on Perfection, and Melanie was number two on Missy.

The girls had decided to go along with Parker's scheme only because it sounded like fun. Christina had dug some of her mother's old racing silks out of the attic. She was wearing blue and white for Whitebrook, and Melanie was wearing gold and green, Townsend Acres' old colors. Parker had invited Samantha and Tor and everyone at Whitebrook to come and watch.

Out in the front paddock Star was trotting along the fence line, his tail up and his hooves barely skimming the ground. The nights had been so balmy that they had begun leaving the mares and foals out all night to graze. Star was so dazzlingly beautiful, Christina's heart surged with pride. No one ever would have guessed that Star had barely survived his own birth and that he'd been so weak and wretched for the first few months of his life. He was the biggest colt at Whitebrook, and Christina couldn't wait until he was old enough to ride—he was really going to be something!

Perfection stood unflinching and serene as ever while Christina tacked him up before their race. Down the aisle, she could hear Missy acting up, as usual.

"Stop that," Melanie cried when Missy began pawing the aisle, her aluminum shoes making a horrible scraping sound on the cement.

"Ready to race?" Christina called to her cousin.

"Ready to win, you mean," her cousin called back, her competitive streak shining through.

"I've got my money on Missy," Kevin called from the barn entrance.

"And I've bet my savings on Perfection," Parker said, winking at Christina.

She blushed. Parker could be so charming sometimes.

"I feel ridiculous in these silks," Christina said self-consciously.

"Well, you look very professional," Parker answered. "And so do you, Melanie."

"Thanks," Melanie answered. "Maybe I should start dressing like this for school," she joked. "Think it might help my grades?"

"Anything would help your grades," Christina commented with a wicked gleam in her eye.

"Hey!" Melanie cried.

"Come on, you two. Save it for the track!" Parker interrupted. "Let's not keep the crowds waiting."

Down by the rail of the training oval Ashleigh, Mike, Samantha, Tor, Naomi, Jonnie, and even George Ballard huddled together, passing doughnuts and coffee between them. Christina glanced at them and then walked Perfection through the gate, her eyes forward, maintaining a professional quietness and poise, just like a real jockey. Out of the corner of her eye she glanced at her cousin. Melanie twisted her face into a mock sneer, as if Christina were her worst enemy, and crouched low in Missy's saddle. It was all Christina could do to keep from bursting into giggles.

They jogged down to the eighth pole to warm up their horses before turning them and jogging back. Parker and Kevin were standing at the starting line, red bandannas in their hands.

"All right," Parker called. "Ready your horses!"

Christina held Perfection at a halt. She could feel his muscles bunching in anticipation of the gallop ahead. She gathered up her reins, crouching low, her chin almost touching Perfection's withers.

Beside them, Melanie circled Missy. The filly jogged in place as Kevin counted down, "Five, four, three, two, one . . ."

"Go!" both boys shouted together.

Perfection leaped forward like a coiled spring, but Missy had a running start and took the lead. Christina's hands pumped with the steady rhythm of Perfection's stride as he galloped on furiously, trying to catch up. Melanie brought Missy close to the rail and stayed put, crouched like a green-and-gold bug on the chestnut's back. Christina dug her knees in and guided Perfection toward the rail, too, closing the gap between the two horses.

Perfection still had a lot more to give, and Christina kept a firm hold on the reins, ready to make a move at the far turn. She was happy to wait, sticking close behind Missy as they galloped around the track, breathing in time to Perfection's stride, reveling in the speed and power of his gallop—and loving every minute of it.

As they came out of the far turn Christina pushed her hands up Perfection's neck and crouched even lower. Perfection surged forward, his neck pumping as he switched into high gear. Ahead of them, Melanie ducked her head under her elbow to judge their speed. She'd heard them coming!

Perfection drew up alongside Missy before shooting past her and into the home stretch. Christina was grinning despite the grit in her teeth—she felt as though she were flying! They sailed past the gate, the little group whooping and cheering as they galloped by.

Christina brought Perfection down to a jog and turned him just as Melanie flew past.

"All right!" her cousin shouted, and Christina gave her a thumbs-up.

When she reached the group by the rail, everyone was grinning and cheering as though she'd actually won the Kentucky Derby.

"You did it!" Parker cried gleefully.

"You look just like your mom up there," Mike said proudly, his arm around Ashleigh.

Ashleigh was wiping her eyes, but she looked thrilled. "I never thought I'd see the day," she murmured.

Christina felt embarrassed. It was only a workout they'd turned into a silly race. What was the big deal?

She turned to wait for her cousin, who was walking

Missy back toward them. The filly tossed her pretty head. Her neck was foamy with lather, but she looked ready to go for another run around the track.

"I'll get you next time," Melanie called, grinning. "Just wait until we're in a real race. I'll beat you every time."

"Right," Christina hooted in a mock competitive tone, hopping to the ground as Parker took Perfection's head. "You'll be eating my dust!" But to herself she scoffed, *As if I would ever be riding in a real race.*

Suddenly, though, the idea didn't seem so ridiculous after all. What if she *did* become a jockey? And what if Star became a racehorse? Maybe they *could* win the Kentucky Derby—for real.

13

THE FOLLOWING SATURDAY, CHRISTINA WORKED STERLING over cavaletti poles in a flat, grassy area next to Whitebrook's biggest pasture. Later on, the whole family was going to watch Missy in her first maiden race, but Christina had just enough time to fit in a good long ride before they went.

Sterling was quiet, listening to Christina's silent aids as she lifted each hoof carefully over the series of twenty poles, which were laid in two rows to form a giant X across the grass. Back and forth they figure-eighted over the poles, first at a trot, then at a canter. A trickle of sweat ran down Christina's neck, and she sat back, loosening her reins and bringing Sterling to a walk so that the mare could rest awhile.

They walked along the pasture fence, where Star was grazing contentedly.

"Hey, boy," Christina called. The colt raised his

head, whinnying at the sound of her voice, and he watched her and Sterling for a moment before lowering his head to graze once more. Since Star had done so well with Raven and Perfect Heart, and all of the colts and fillies were eating grass now, Ashleigh and Mike had decided to put Star out in the pasture with all the other foals and their dams.

Christina halted Sterling to gaze at her colt for a moment. Star's gleaming neck was stretched out as far as it would go, his legs straddled so he could reach the sweet grass. He was eating busily, but every now and then he would look up, quietly surveying the group of horses with his intelligent, amber-flecked eyes. He was like a little stallion, responsible for the safety and happiness of his herd.

Christina sighed and picked up her reins, squeezing her inside leg to bend Sterling around it. But she didn't really feel like working Sterling anymore. In fact, she wished she could be riding Star. She turned Sterling and let the mare amble slowly back to the barn, glancing now and then to admire how pretty Star looked, eating clover in the sunshine.

The track was already bustling, though there were still two hours left before the first race. It had been months since Christina had gone to the races with her family, but she felt right at home as soon as she followed her mother through the gate to the backside, where the

136

horses were stabled. Everywhere she looked, walkers were leading tall, sleek Thoroughbreds. Some of the horses had brightly colored sheets draped over their backs with matching bandages wrapped around their lower legs. Others had been bathed and brushed until their coats gleamed. All were lean and racing fit, their muscles holding the power to run as fast as the wind.

"Let's find Naomi and Missy," Melanie said, grabbing Christina's sleeve.

"Mike said they're in barn three. You girls go on ahead. There are some people I want to talk to," Ashleigh said, waving them on. She was wearing her trainer clothes—crisp khakis and a blue blazer. Racing days were business days for her, because she had to spend them talking with other owners and trainers.

Christina sniffed appreciatively as they made their way down the sawdust walks in front of the barns. Liniment and horse shampoo mingled with the sweet scents of saddle soap and hay to make her favorite perfume. Excitement permeated the air in the soft murmurs of grooms readying their horses, the hearty laughs of owners inspecting their investments, and the solemn nods of small, sharp-faced jockeys listening to trainers in flat hats or battered straw fedoras give instructions.

"There she is," Melanie said, pointing to the orange chestnut with a pretty dished face.

Missy was looking around with interest as Jonnie blackened her hooves with dressing. She didn't seem at all disturbed by the excitement around her.

"Hi, Jonnie. How's she behaving?" Christina asked as she ran her hand down Missy's neck. The filly's coat felt like silk under her fingers.

Jonnie grunted as he straightened up. "Couldn't be better. She's handling everything like a pro. Go figure." He patted the filly's hindquarters before bending down again to do her back feet.

"Are you going to win your first race?" Melanie said in a baby-talk voice. The filly raised her muzzle and blew against Melanie's cheek. Christina could see that during the time Melanie had spent exercising and training the horse, she and Missy had forged a special bond. In another year Melanie could be racing Missy herself— what a team they would make!

Melanie began to put the finishing touches on Missy while Joe brought Touch of Class out of her stall. It seemed as though everybody but Christina had a job.

"Where are Dad and Naomi?" Christina asked, unsure of what to do with herself.

"Mike's with the blacksmith," Joe said, putting the lid back onto the can of gooey hoof dressing, "and Naomi caught some last-minute rides with Avenel Farm. She's talking to the trainer now."

"I guess I'll go look around some," Christina said. She made her way down the aisle, stopping to pat the horses who looked sociable and steering clear of the ones who pinned their ears back and ground their teeth as she approached. Townsend Acres had horses running that day, too. Christina recognized the gold-and-green striped setup along six stalls in the next barn down. *Are they going to have any horses in Missy's race?* she wondered, wishing she had picked up a program on the way in.

Melanie caught up with her on her way to find a program. "You want to get something to eat before the race?" she asked. "I'm starving."

By the time Christina got to the front of the long line at the snack bar, the smell of the seasoned fries had made her hungry, too. With cheeseburgers and sodas in hand, they made their way to the shade of the grandstand to eat.

"I might as well enjoy this while I can," Melanie said, poking the pickle back under the bun of her ketchup-drenched burger. "I'm going to have to stop eating this kind of stuff when I'm a jockey."

Christina laughed as her cousin tried to cram the oversized sandwich into her mouth. "You eat like this now and you're still a stick," she pointed out.

"True," Melanie said after she'd swallowed. "Maybe I won't have to starve myself after all."

Christina only half listened as her cousin chattered about all the special diets jockeys went on. She was thinking about Star. He seemed to be ahead of the game now, since the other foals were going to be weaned from their dams in a few weeks, and that always caused a major upset. She wondered how Star would react to a field of screaming colts and fillies, all desperate for their mothers. Star had felt that way from day one!

A gray Thoroughbred jogged by below them. Christina could tell he was favoring his back leg. *Too bad*, she thought idly.

A tall older man in a gray flat cap went up to the horse and ran his hand down the animal's back leg. Something about the man looked familiar.

When he straightened and turned so Christina could see his face, she recognized him at last. It was Parker's grandfather, Clay Townsend.

She hadn't known Mr. Townsend was back from Europe. *I wonder if he'll come to see Star,* she mused. Wonder and her offspring had done their part to put Townsend Acres on the map—surely Clay Townsend would want to see what Wonder's last foal looked like, even if his son thought Star was a dud.

By the time the girls joined Mike and Ashleigh in their seats, the post parade for Missy's race was about to begin.

"There she is. Number four," Melanie said as the two-year-olds filed onto the track.

Christina could tell by the way Missy's mouth was foaming up around the bit that she was a lot more keyed up than she had been on the backside. When Missy bumped into the horse that was ponying her, leaving a big white splatter of foam on his hindquarters, Christina couldn't help but smile. *Same old Missy,* she thought.

The starters loaded the horses into the gate in number order. Christina was proud of the way Missy walked right into the narrow starting stall without a fight. Ashleigh and Mike spent a lot of time training Whitebrook's horses so they wouldn't be scared of the barrier.

Everything was going like clockwork until they got to the last horse, a bay colt who was doing his best to stay away from the gate. Finally four starters working together got him inside, but Christina gasped when the colt went up on his hind legs. She didn't know how the jockey managed to stay on, but a second later the bar was latched behind him, and an instant after that the front doors snapped open. They were off!

It was hard to spot Missy in the clump of horses vying for the lead, but when a chestnut dropped back, splitting from the group, Christina recognized Naomi's blue-and-white silks.

"Good. She's moving to the outside," Melanie yelled in her ear.

It was the long way around, and Naomi wasn't going to risk pushing Missy out in front too soon. Since it was Missy's first time out, Naomi had been told to play it on the safe side in case the filly tried anything unexpected. Three horses pulled away in front, leaving Missy in fourth place as they swept into the turn.

"That's it," Ashleigh said, talking Naomi through the race all the way from the grandstand. "Give her some space so she can figure it out."

On the backstretch the three lead horses began to spread out, with Julius in the lead and Switchback and

Ten for Ten close behind. Missy drifted back toward the inside rail but kept her spot in the center of the pack. Christina kept expecting Naomi to push her on and close the distance around the second turn, but the chestnut just followed on behind as though she were in a checkout line, politely waiting her turn. Christina squeezed her hands into tight fists around imaginary reins. She couldn't help herself—she wanted to be out there riding, too!

As the two-year-olds came down the final stretch, Julius bobbled and drifted to the right, opening the race up for the other horses. Ten for Ten took advantage of the opportunity and was just creeping past Switchback on the outside when Naomi made her move.

"Yes," Melanie shouted. "Go get 'em, girl!"

Steadily Missy gained on them, coming up on the inside of Switchback just as he began to drift left.

"They're going to crash," Christina cried. But Switchback's jockey waved his whip and swerved right again, leaving just enough room for Missy next to the rail. Soon Missy and Switchback had caught up with Ten for Ten, and it was three horses, neck and neck, pounding down the track to the finish. Christina couldn't tell whose nose was in front as they swept past the finish pole.

"Who won?" she asked as her father lowered his binoculars.

"It's a photo finish," Mike said, shaking his head, his eyes shining. But Christina knew that no matter what the outcome was, Missy had done very well for her first race.

Everyone was silent as they waited for the results of the race. Finally the announcer called out the results. "And the winner of the fifth race, for maiden two-year-olds, is number four, Mischief Maker!"

"We won! We won!" Melanie grabbed Christina and squeezed her in a bear hug as Christina let out a shout of celebration.

"Aren't you glad you came?" Ashleigh asked, grabbing Christina's hand and pulling her toward the winner's circle.

As Christina started down the steps she saw Mr. Townsend wave from the railing in front of the grandstand. Ashleigh waved back, mouthing the words, *I'll call you*. Then she and Christina continued down to the winner's circle to be with Missy and Naomi.

Well, Christina thought as they picked their way through the crowd, *if Mom and Dad didn't know Mr. Townsend was back in town, they know now*. Christina told herself she had nothing to worry about—after all, Brad must have told his father what he thought of Star. Lurking in the back of her mind, though, was the silent fear that once Brad and Clay Townsend saw that Star was no dud, they might want to keep him for themselves.

Melanie decided to stay at the track with Naomi, and Mike had a late dinner meeting with a prospective buyer, so Christina and Ashleigh headed back to Whitebrook after the last race. It was quiet in the car after the commotion of the racetrack.

Ashleigh broke the silence first. "Pretty exciting day, huh?"

"Yeah," Christina said.

"I wasn't sure Missy would be able to handle the pressure of the track, but she ran that race like a real pro. Of course, Naomi did a good job of keeping her out of trouble."

This was the way it always was driving home from the track, with her mother going over each race in as much detail as if she'd been the one riding. Christina's mind wandered.

By the time Star was two years old, Melanie would have her jockey's license—or her apprentice one, anyway. Would her cousin get to ride Star in his first race? Two years from now, would they be rehashing Star's performance as they drove home?

Christina tried to picture Star in the winner's circle: a tall, coppery chestnut with a heart-shaped white star. When he finished growing, he'd be even bigger than Sterling. Already he looked months ahead of the other foals in the barn, even though he was just a few weeks older. And he was smart, too. Christina could see it in his eyes.

Christina's mind went back to the image of Star in the winner's circle. Would that be his destiny? Or would she be able to figure out a way to keep Star to train and ride in the Olympics?

The realization that Ashleigh had stopped speaking and was waiting expectantly for an answer brought Christina back to the present.

"Well, weren't you?" her mother prompted.

"What?" Christina answered, confused.

"Weren't you proud? After all, you were the one who first handled Missy."

Christina shrugged. "I guess so." If her mother noticed Christina's preoccupation, she didn't let on.

"I remember Wonder's first race." Ashleigh's eyes were on the road, but her voice sounded far away. "It was at Churchill Downs, the hottest day in July. The other jockeys were giving us a hard time because Wonder's jockey wasn't carrying a whip."

Christina nodded. She'd heard all about Wonder's fear of whips. Ashleigh was the one who had restored Wonder's confidence and proved the mare had the heart to race without one.

"Wonder drew the number six position," Ashleigh continued. "And even though she got boxed in early in the race, when the jockey asked her for more, Wonder just took off. I thought Brad Townsend was going to explode when Wonder came from behind like that. He never had any faith in her. We showed him, all right, and all the other people who were trying to write Wonder off. She ran a great race. She had so much heart—I loved her so much," Ashleigh continued softly. Christina had the feeling her mother had forgotten she was there.

"That's exactly how I feel about Star," Christina

said, eager to share her love for the colt with her mother. But Ashleigh's face went blank, and she didn't answer.

"What's wrong?" Christina demanded.

But Ashleigh remained silent.

"Mom, what's going to happen to Star? And why won't you talk about him?"

Ashleigh's hands tightened on the steering wheel. "I don't know what we're going to do with Star," she answered, ignoring her daughter's second question.

"*Why* don't you know?" Christina demanded. "You know about Raven, and Catwink, and River, and Rumba," she said, reeling off the names of the other spring foals. "And you always do this. Every time I try to talk about Star, you change the subject or leave the room. Why? What's wrong with him?" The words tumbled out of Christina's mouth before she could stop them.

Ashleigh took a deep breath, but she pressed her lips together and remained silent. Christina stared at her profile, waiting.

"Aren't you going to answer?" she demanded finally.

Her mother's lip trembled. "Not now. I can't talk about it right now."

Fine, Christina thought, slumping in the seat.

They rode the rest of the way back to Whitebrook in silence.

14

TWO WEEKS PASSED IN A BLUR OF EARLY-MORNING EXERCISE riding, writing end-of-term papers for school, going for long hacks on Sterling with Parker, and taking leisurely walks with Star in the pasture. Finally the day to wean Whitebrook's other colts and fillies arrived, and Christina was enlisted to help.

One by one Jonnie and Mike led the foals out of their stalls. The young horses went willingly, assuming their mothers would follow right behind them, but when the gate of the paddock clicked shut and the foals looked around, their mothers were gone.

In the barn, the mares began to whinny nervously for their babies, but the full weight of what was happening hadn't yet hit them.

Christina led Star out right behind Raven, hoping his presence would help soothe the filly. The black filly

147

danced in front of them, turning her head coyly to nicker at Star.

"What a flirt," Mike said with a chuckle, leading Raven through the gate. Christina latched it behind Star, and they leaned against the fence, watching to see what would happen once the horses realized that their mothers had been left behind.

A big, seal-brown colt named Rumba let out a high-pitched, sorrowful scream, and from the barn his mother whinnied back, the sound desperate and short. Suddenly the air was filled with the resounding cries of babies calling for their mothers. *Where are you? Where are you?* their whinnies seemed to say.

Christina remembered when Star had sounded the same way, calling for her or Nana. Star had been forced to grow up fast, since he had gone without a real mother his whole life, and now he was acting as though he didn't know what all the fuss was about. While the other foals were running up and down the fence searching for their mothers, Star stood stock still in the middle of the pasture, watching quietly as if trying to decide what to do.

Suddenly Star whirled around on his hind legs, breaking into a canter and circling back toward the group of young horses. They responded by clustering together and beginning to canter themselves as he chased them. Star lowered his head, increasing his pace and waving his nose at the stragglers. Then he galloped past the group, a copper streak on the thick Kentucky bluegrass. The young horses took off after him, their mothers forgotten in their eager pursuit. It looked as though Star had his own herd of admirers—the colt was a natural-born leader.

"That's a lovely colt you've raised, Christina." Clay Townsend's gravelly voice boomed from behind her.

Christina whirled around to see Brad and Clay Townsend standing side by side with her mother. She smiled at Clay—he had always been kind to her—and ignored Brad altogether.

"Parker told me all about the struggle you've had with him, but it looks like the hard times are over. Well done," Clay went on.

"Thank you," Christina said, beaming proudly.

"He's obviously Wonder's boy," Brad commented, gazing at Star admiringly.

Well, Brad's sure changed his tune, Christina scoffed inwardly.

"That he is," Clay agreed. "He's got her spirit and her intelligence."

"You can pick him up as soon as you like," Ashleigh told him.

Christina stared at her mother. *Pick him up? What does she mean?* Her mother wouldn't send Star to Townsend Acres, would she?

"I'll send Parker by with the trailer tomorrow, if that's all right," Clay answered.

Christina felt as though the earth had dropped out from beneath her, and she had to close her eyes to keep her balance. *The Townsends are going to take Star away?*

Her father wrapped his arm around her shoulder, but Christina shrugged his arm away. Numb with horror, she watched as Ashleigh and Clay shook hands, and Clay and Brad turned to leave. Christina's hands balled up in fists, and frustrated tears sprang into her eyes.

"What is going on?" she demanded. Her mouth had gone dry.

Ashleigh came over to stand near Christina and gestured at the foals still milling about in the paddock. "You can see that we have more young horses here than we can manage," she said. "Townsend Acres has more room and more staff, and they've just weaned six of their foals, so Star can be turned out with them," she added, as if it were a perfectly reasonable explanation.

"You're giving Star to the Townsends?" Christina asked. Even as she said it, she couldn't believe that this was happening. "But why? Why don't you want him?" Christina demanded, her voice trembling. "Can't you see he's all right now? Look." She pointed to where Star stood grazing beside Raven. "He's just like all the other foals."

But her mother didn't turn to look. Her face was pale in the bright sunlight as she stared at Christina intently. "He's *not* like all the others, Christina," she said. "You know it and I know it. He's Wonder's orphan, and every time I look at him, I remember."

Christina stared at her mother. So *now* she knew

150

why Ashleigh hated Star. "So you called the Townsends and asked them to come take him away?" she asked bitterly.

Ashleigh shook her head. "You know as well as we do that any foal of Wonder's is half owned by Townsend Acres. I called Clay because he has as much right to decide what to do with Star as we do. This works best for everyone."

Angry tears sprang to Christina's eyes "Not for *me*!" she cried. "Not for Star!" Couldn't her mother see that Star was too precious to split in half? Star was *hers*. How would he survive without her? How would she live without him?

"Christina, we know you had other plans—" her father started, but Christina cut him off, glaring at her mother.

"You're just making excuses to send Star away because you blame him for Wonder's death." Her words came out like daggers, but she didn't care. How could she, after what her mother had done?

Ashleigh grimaced and looked away.

"He'll be better off at Townsend Acres," Mike said, squeezing Christina's shoulders. She squirmed away.

"How?" Christina sobbed. "How can he be better off? Why would you let them take Wonder's last baby? It doesn't make any sense!" Tears spilled down her cheeks as she bolted past her mother, her mind racing.

She couldn't let them take Star away.

She wouldn't.

Christina sprinted to the house, intent on locking herself in her room forever. But on the porch she stopped. She didn't want to be inside. What she really needed was to get away!

She stumbled down the porch steps, her tears blurring the ground in front of her, and ran across the yard, through the gap in the fence, and into the shade of the woods beyond. Her breath came in sharp, uneven gasps as she cried and ran, but she didn't slow down until her sides ached too much to go any further.

Christina stayed there, sitting at the base of a tree and crying, until the shadows grew long and a coolness filled the breeze that rustled the leaves. Finally she heard the familiar shouts and whinnies of feeding time, and then the bang of the screen door as her parents went into the house.

Now she could be alone with Star.

Christina worked her way back toward the stallion barn, staying in its shadow until she reached the edge of the broodmare barn. Inside, Star was waiting in his stall, unaware that his small world was about to be shaken once again.

She crossed the lighted barnyard and slipped inside the open barn doors, giving her eyes a moment to adjust to the dark before she headed for Star's stall. She felt for the latch and slowly slid the bolt open. Next door, Sterling shifted, breathing deeply. At Christina's feet, a dark shadow was sprawled across the straw. Star was lying down.

"It's okay, boy. It's just me," she whispered.

Star lifted his head and nickered softly. Christina closed the door behind her and tiptoed across the stall.

"Hey, Star," she said, kneeling by his head. She ran her finger along his muzzle, loving the velvety softness. Star breathed deeply, and she could feel the flutter of warm air across her hand. Then the colt stretched out in the straw, sighing sleepily as he rested his head in Christina's lap. She remembered the last time he'd slept like that—the night Wonder died.

How can they send you away? Christina asked silently. *How can they take you away from me?*

Why couldn't her mother see that Christina loved Star as much as Ashleigh had loved Wonder? Everyone else had wanted to give up on the sickly filly all those years ago. But Ashleigh hadn't listened. She had stood up for Wonder.

And now Christina had to stand up for Star.

15

THE HOUSE WAS STILL WHEN SHE WENT INSIDE. THE KITCHEN light was on, but the room was empty. Christina crossed the floor and peeked around the door to the living room. It was empty, too. She was about to turn around and go upstairs to her bedroom when a sound caught her ear—a cough, or a sob.

Her feet were silent on the braided rug as she walked into the living room. Then she heard the noise again. It *was* the sound of someone crying. And it was coming from her mother's office next door.

When Christina pushed the door open, she saw her mother sitting cross-legged on the floor, her shoulders shaking, her hair covering her face as she studied a photo album lying open in her lap. Scattered around her in a circle were photographs of Wonder.

"Mom?"

Ashleigh scrambled to her knees, turning away so her face was hidden. "What?"

Christina stepped into the room. "Are you okay?"

Ashleigh nodded as she snatched up a box of tissues from her desk. The corner of the box caught the side of a framed picture standing on the edge of the desk. Ashleigh made a grab for it, but she missed, and the glass shattered as it hit the hardwood floor.

Her mother sank down again, openly crying as she tried to pick up the pieces of glass.

"Let me help," Christina said, grabbing the wastebasket and kneeling down beside her mother. Ashleigh didn't protest until Christina tried to take the broken picture with the loose shards of glass out of her hand. Her mother's fingers tightened on the silver frame and she wouldn't let go.

Christina had always loved that picture. It was a photograph of her mother and Wonder, not in the winner's circle of a racetrack but standing in the knee-high grass of a field that hadn't been hayed yet. Ashleigh was in cutoffs, stretched out along Wonder's back with her arms around the mare's neck, which gleamed like a copper penny in the sunshine. Wonder's ears were forward as she stared into the distance, and the camera had caught her tail in midswish.

"It was taken the day after Wonder won the Breeders' Cup and Clay Townsend gave her to me." Ashleigh's voice was unsteady. "I knew I was the luckiest person in the world."

"She was a great horse," Christina said, but her mother went on as if she hadn't heard.

"At first I loved her because she needed me. She made up for all the horses my family had lost when we had to sell our farm and move to the Townsends'." Ashleigh took a deep breath. "But then I found out that I needed her more. She was so brave and she had so much heart . . . and look what I did to her!" she sobbed.

Christina paused, crouched awkwardly with the wastebasket in one hand and a piece of glass in the other. She didn't know what to say—she wasn't sure what her mother was talking about. *She didn't do anything to Wonder*, Christina thought. *She tried to save her, but Wonder was too sick.*

"Mom . . . ," she finally began.

Ashleigh put her hand to her mouth as if she was in pain. "Don't you see? I killed her by breeding her one last time. If it hadn't been for me, Wonder would still be alive."

The despair in her mother's voice brought tears to Christina's eyes. "That's not true," she protested. "You always said she was happiest when she was a mother. It wasn't your fault she died."

Ashleigh shook her head. "She was too old. I should have seen the signs."

"But you did everything you could," Christina insisted.

Ashleigh clutched her head, shaking it and sobbing even harder. "Oh, Chris, I know it's awful to say, but I can't bear it—every time I turn around, that colt is there, reminding me."

Christina hated seeing her mother so distraught, but she had come here to defend Star, hadn't she? Before she had a chance to say anything, though, her mother went on.

"And now you hate me because I'm sending him to Townsend Acres. And you're right—I'm doing it because every time I see Star, it feels like a knife is turning in my chest!"

Christina's lip trembled as she realized the weight of the burden Ashleigh had been carrying all these months. Tears streamed down her cheeks as she reached out to hug her mother tightly. "I *don't* hate you," she sobbed. She held her mother for a moment before Ashleigh pulled back to gaze into Christina's face. The absolute misery in her mother's eyes told Christina what she had to do.

"I think Star will be happier there," she lied, fighting back the lump that rose in her throat and threatened to choke her.

Ashleigh studied her, as if giving Christina the chance to change her mind. And even though her heart was breaking, Christina stood firm.

"Thank you," Ashleigh said softly, her voice full of relief, as if a terrible weight had been lifted from her. She wrapped her arms around Christina, hugging her close, and while the thought of sending Star away was almost unbearable, Christina knew she'd done the right thing.

• • •

That night Christina sat sideways in the window seat in her room, unable to sleep.

The full moon's light passed through the window-panes, turning her rug into a giant checkerboard. It was a beautiful night. Something on the hill behind the barns caught her eye, and Christina squinted, a lump rising to her throat as she recognized Wonder's grave, standing out like an ugly scab in the grass. Suddenly Christina was overcome with guilt for never having visited the grave. It looked so bare and forlorn.

Christina rose and went downstairs, closing the screen door quietly behind her as she stepped out onto the front porch. She pulled down two of Ashleigh's hanging pots of red geraniums, sure that her mother wouldn't mind. Wonder deserved more than a bare spot of earth in the field—Christina wanted to make her grave beautiful.

The grass was moist with dew under her bare feet as she headed through the pasture and up the hill to the grave site. There, by the light of the moon, Christina planted the flowers in a neat semicircle, like a horse-shoe.

When she was done, she rocked back on her heels. A light breeze stirred the flowers, but the pasture was quiet.

"Pretty red flowers, Wonder," she whispered, breaking the silence. "Just like you won at the Kentucky

Derby." Far off, a barn owl hooted, as if in response. Christina sat still, taking in the sweet smell of spring grass on a warm night. And then she began to tell Wonder all about Star, her beautiful colt.

The plan was that Parker would drive Star to Townsend Acres, Christina riding with him in his pickup. But when it was time to load Star into the trailer, Christina knew she couldn't go.

Feeling numb, she tugged on the lead rope, and the chestnut colt followed her willingly across the barnyard to the trailer's ramp, where her father and Parker were waiting. Ashleigh had stayed in the house—she felt bad enough that she was sending Star away—and Christina understood.

"Do you want me to lead him in?" Mike asked.

Star had never been near a trailer before, so loading him wasn't going to be easy.

"Sure," Christina said dully, handing her father the lead rope.

"We'll get behind him," Parker offered.

But when Star saw that Mike wanted him to go in the trailer, his head shot up and he planted his feet, refusing to budge. Christina watched anxiously as Mike patted the colt's neck and tightened his grasp on the lead rope. "Come on, boy, you can do it," he coaxed, walking forward.

Star rolled his eyes in fright as he backed away,

nearly yanking the lead rope out of Mike's hands. "Whoa," Mike called. "Easy, boy."

Christina took a step forward, and her father held out the lead rope. "Here, Chris. I think it's better if you do it. He'll go on for you."

Christina took the rope back and reached up to rub Star's forehead. "I know, Star," she said softly. "I don't want you to go, either."

She leaned into him, burying her face in his soft mane and taking in his sweet horsy scent for the last time. Star dipped his head, nuzzling her back as if to soothe her, and Christina fought back the tears that had been threatening to fall all morning.

She took a deep breath and glanced up at her father and Parker, who were watching her worriedly. *I can do this*, she told herself. *It's not as though I'll never see Star again. I can visit him at Townsend Acres, and Parker will be there to keep an eye on him.*

"Come on, boy," she said, pulling away to pat Star's neck. "You'll be all right."

Christina turned back to the trailer, hating the way it gaped at her like a big mouth ready to swallow Star up forever. But she knew that Star would stop again if she hesitated, so she kept walking without looking back. Behind her, she could feel Star taking small, nervous steps, trusting her as he followed her up the ramp and into the trailer.

Mike and Parker raised and bolted the ramp and Christina clipped the trailer ties onto Star's halter with trembling fingers. She looked up into Star's sweet, intelligent eyes, a sob choking her as the tears began to fall at last.

She wanted to shrink him and put him in her room, to keep him for herself forever, like a stuffed bear. But Star was a Thoroughbred with a racing career ahead of him. In a year's time, would he even remember who she was?

Parker peered into the little doorway at the front of the trailer, and Christina stepped back.

"Ready?" he asked gently.

Christina nodded, and Parker held out his hand to help her down from the trailer. Christina buried her face in his shoulder. "I can't go. I'm staying here," she sobbed.

"That's all right," Parker soothed, rubbing her back. "I'll take care of him. He'll be all right."

"I'll close the door," her father announced, and Christina was grateful. It would be worse if she could see Star's face peeking out the door when she turned around.

The door clicked shut. Inside, Star whinnied and stamped his foot in alarm.

The driveway seemed to be spinning as Christina turned and called out to him. "I'm right here, Star."

Star whinnied again, more desperately now, and Parker squeezed her hand. "I'd better get going before he makes a fuss," he said.

Christina nodded and backed away, crossing her

arms over her chest as she watched Parker hop into his truck and start the ignition. Star's cries rang out through the air, each one wrenching at her heart.

Christina and Mike watched as the trailer pulled away slowly with Star inside, off to be raised and trained by strangers.

What will happen to him? Christina wondered desperately. *What am I going to do now?*

Parker's truck and trailer turned down the road and disappeared from sight.

To her right, Christina could see her mother watching from the porch, all alone. Mike wrapped his arm around Christina's shoulders, steering her gently toward the house. As they walked, a solitary foal cried out for his mother from the paddock. Then the farm fell eerily silent.

One thing Christina was sure of: Whitebrook would never, ever be the same.

THOROUGHBRED

If you enjoyed this book, then you'll love reading all the books in the THOROUGHBRED series!

THOROUGHBRED

**All books are
$4.50 U.S./$5.50 Canadian**